7u3 3

WILD
NIGHTS

WILD
NIGHTS

EMMA TENNANT

JONATHAN CAPE
THIRTY BEDFORD SQUARE LONDON

First published 1979
© 1979 by Emma Tennant

Jonathan Cape Ltd, 30 Bedford Square, London WC1

British Library Cataloguing in Publication Data

Tennant, Emma
Wild nights.
I. Title
823'.9'1F   PR6070.E52W/
ISBN 0-224-01708-X

Printed in Great Britain by The Anchor Press Ltd
and bound by Wm Brendon & Son Ltd
both of Tiptree, Essex

For Colin

PART ONE
North

WHEN my aunt Zita came, there were changes every-where. The days outside, which were long and white at that time of year, closed and turned like a shutter, a sharp blue night coming on sudden and unexpected as a finger caught in a hinge. The house shrank; the walls seemed to lean inwards; my mother's shoulders grew hunched, as if she were trying to ward off some weight that was bound to descend from above. The people in the house were as sensitive as oysters. As they turned to look at each other, or if they brushed past each other in the long corridors, they trembled and their eyes ran. Caught by this new early night, so unlike the slow stealthy evenings which up till then had removed trees one by one and hidden the house only after everyone was safely inside – the women who were helping my mother make Aunt Zita's bed stumbled against corners, lost their feet on a bottomless floor, swore as they pressed the switch to make the light come on. Then the night outside mocked them, once they had made its presence official, by turning a pale, innocent blue like a hedge-sparrow's egg. But even to run out into it was to be tricked again. The shadows under the trees were as black and rich as the feathers in Aunt Zita's hats.

In spite of all this, my father paid no attention to the changes and sat over his papers in his study. He had had to put on the light, and by doing so he had ended the summer. He had bundled the long days, the dog days when the grass begins to show yellow and the haystacks slip over to one side, into one of the drawers of his enormous desk. They disintegrated there, amongst the faded legal documents: a north wind came down from the hills and my father pinched his nose. He did this when he was pleased. And he was pleased, of course, that Aunt Zita was coming, on that cold shudder of air from the mountains. He must have thought of the games they had played together in the winter, in the cold rooms upstairs when the freezing air played a Tom Tiddler's with them, and sent them running to beds and chairs for shelter. Even now, with my mother's face drawn and her eyes agonised and lifeless like the eyes of a toy animal, he had to assume a frozen look at the coming of Aunt Zita. He had to hide his old love for her. But he was unable to stop himself from pinching his nose. And my mother, with those dead, staring eyes, suffered in silence as, unaware, he demonstrated his emotions.

The window of my father's study was square, and a bright red since he had turned on the light. Round it the rest of the house was unrecognisable. The walls and turrets – all of them unoccupied – of the mock castle his grandfather had built seemed to hang in folds, uncertain, waiting for the new season, for the advent of Aunt Zita. The evening wind puffed a few leaves from the rowan tree by the door, but they went out of sight before they reached the ground. Other windows of rooms long empty shone in their own way, by reflecting the new moon, and ghosts began to get ready for Aunt Zita in these dusty rooms full of dead flies. After she had eaten the ordinary food with my mother and father, she would go up and be with them. I had seen her on a window sill, with the moon shining straight in on her. When I couldn't sleep, I heard their skirts rustling on the floor above.

Some of the summer was still trapped in the wide, grassy

path that led down to the house from the hills. From the path, which still smelt of day and dying flowers, the house looked as it normally did. It hadn't yet swelled in the upper storeys to accommodate the ghostly maids. The turrets, which had always been despised by Aunt Zita, were not small and cross-eyed. The house basked in the endless, white days of the falling summer. But the summer was false. Aunt Zita and the north wind together had ended it. Even on the path, with its last traces of summer, my mother now walked with an autumnal, anxious step. Once she had gazed up at the sky, which was always darker over the hills. Now on the shaved, yellow grass of the path she went with short steps and head down.

When the grass path, wide as a drove road, had passed the house it grew narrow and went down over several banks towards the fields and the chicken-house. The uncut grass on either side was very long, and people who walked on the path could only be seen from the shoulders up, like people standing in a boat and being carried downstream by the current. Strangers who had wandered in their walks on the hills and lost their way, turned up in these grassy canals and found themselves at the house before being rescued and pulled out, set on the road to the mouth of the valley. Their frightened eyes danced about like bees just above the level of the coarse grass. Over them, as they flowed in and out of the maze, stood the stone guns and flying buttresses of mid-nineteenth-century capitalism. They heard the machinery, the turning wheels of my uncle's latest invention as he strove, year after year, to turn the whole edifice around so that it would dance on a pivot like an elephant on a ball. Then, if he had succeeded, the house might have opened up to them too – and they would have seen my father in his study, and my mother in her bedroom, stepping in and out of her cupboard with dresses sealed in bags, and Aunt Zita unpacking in a front room that never caught the sun. Pale women, known only to Aunt Zita, would be found coughing in four-poster beds, and over their heads, exposed shamelessly to the air, wreaths of faded willow leaves and berries the colour of dried blood. The money that had built the great revolving house, and the iron dust in the air, and the thick curtains and sinuous drapery which had more vigour than the women who lived among them, had killed the daughters of the house. But the strangers saw only a great monument to the Industrial Revolution. My uncle's invention had no more strength than a sewing machine, and a good deal more frivolity.

Maurice was often down by the chicken-house. He had told me many times that an old man lived in the house with the hens, and he showed me human turds in the yard to prove it. He picked them up and rolled them in his hands, and pointed to the chicken shit, smaller and lighter in colour. He danced and jumped on the rubbish dump, which was made up out of old nettles and which, in the long, dry days of summer, fermented and returned to slime. The smell of the chickens and the rubbish dump sealed off the little patch, so that people coming up to it or going away seemed to walk in a haze, like the dancing air from jet engines, or the shimmer of mirage. Forests of willow-herb grew round the dump and the low, wooden hen-house. Like pointed flames they pressed in the desolate area round the run. If Aunt Zita and my mother went down there, they looked at the willow-herb and then looked away again, although in the upper garden they spoke approvingly of the flowers. They smelt, probably, the insecure ground from which these aggressive plants drew their strength: the stones and undernourished earth beneath. They saw the rubbish dump, with the latest handful of nettles on top in a lurching crown: they feared for their shoes, that the polished leather which came down with a hiss on the chicken shit might be overcome by the rubbish and pulled from their feet with a squelch. They never saw the old man in the hut. Aunt Zita went in once, bending very low, but she came out with the china egg, the egg they give hens to help them in their laying, and in her anger she threw it down on the muddy ground. The old man, crouching on a slatted shelf, must have seen her face come in like a moon. Round him the chickens clucked and pecked, and he could no longer tell their sounds apart from the rumblings of his stomach. He was thin and scraggy as an old cockerel. She must have seen darkness in the back of the hut, and a few feathers, the white hairs over the muddy scalp of the old man.

Maurice hid in a tall yew tree behind the chicken-house when Aunt Zita and my mother came to see the hens. It was often a sunny day; he would hang in the tree above his shadow; and when they turned to go he ran down the beautiful tree like a monkey until the round black head of his shadow sank into the ground. After it was dark he led me up the narrow path to the house, but he never came in. I only saw him there once, away from the farm above the house or the chicken-run below it. Night, and a bright sky, with the house filled by Aunt Zita and her whispering companions, and I went to the window to look out at the hill and the whiteness, brittle as icing sugar, which had always gone by morning. Maurice stood under the window. He was staring up at us, but the stone of the house must have seemed lighter, more penetrable than our extinguished windows like the pupils of eyes, grown blind and gigantic, swimming behind glass.

The willow-herb, stagily lit by the stars, stood in a great army round him. Perhaps Maurice always walked with them at night. Aunt Zita opened her window and leaned out, and they stretched up towards her, like swords.

Evening had settled in, bringing a new darkness to the house, a darkness that came only with Aunt Zita. The lamps lost nearly all of their power, the light that came out from behind their careful shades made the eyes strain, and my mother said, sighing on a sofa where she was hardly visible:

'Isn't it dim?'

My father walked about at the end of the room. Bottles on a tray stood waiting for Aunt Zita. The house was cold, and apart from the distant clattering of the ghostly maids – which my father and mother pretended not to hear – it was quiet as a valley where the stream has slowly dried up. Soon, in fact, we began to notice the lack of the sound of water outside. The spring from the mountains, which turned into a river, then a waterfall, and then, directed to a dynamo, made our electricity in a glass house down by the chicken-run, was no longer going through the garden, making a sound of rushing wind, of stones knocking against the damp reeds on either side. The house and the garden were dark and dry. My mother sat helplessly, in the shrinking circle of light. My father went to open the sitting-room door, to look out for Aunt Zita. The bottles stood behind him, and behind them books bound in leather and gold, seldom opened, where the words and the stale paper of the pages, if prised apart, gave off a strong smell.

Aunt Zita came into the room, for the first time since her arrival on the doorstep, and the faint, flickering blue flame that had played round her then had become stronger in colour, tinged with red at the tips like a fire-bearing bird. Her face was pale ... as she was continually consumed and resurrected by the flames she lived bloodlessly amongst them ... and her lips, a dead magenta colour, were always smiling. My mother went over to greet her. My father mixed a drink, which Aunt Zita took with a hand so white

14

that it looked painted. My mother and father both knew the lights would go out altogether in a few moments. Their inner voices struggled to reach each other, with a mixture of anger and reassurance, but Aunt Zita lay between them like a bar of static electricity. They all moved back to the sofa, as if the drinks they were holding led them there. The lights went out. My mother gave a little moan.

'I said it was dim. And now the lights have gone out. How extraordinary, Zita, this happened the last time you came!'

My poor mother! She still lived in the age of cause and consequence, of foreshadowings and outcomes, and she couldn't see the connections between Aunt Zita and the fading lights. My father, who was a century ahead of his brother Ralph but was still firmly rooted in the mechanical age, said:

'The dynamo's been clogged by leaves again, I'm afraid. We'll have to hope that Willie's going down to see to it tonight.'

'I always feel it's too dangerous to go down there at night,' said my mother.

Throughout all this Aunt Zita sat quite demurely with her drink on the edge of the sofa. The logs in the hearth, encouraged by her presence, stirred, gave off a few sparks, and then slumped together again. Aunt Zita's fire burned on, a frill of yellow and poppy-red, playing round her face and down the sides of her white dress. Her fire was like one of those natural but magical phenomena, the wandering flame on a marsh. But my mother and father, bumping into one another in the doorway, fetching paraffin lamps, saw nothing at all.

At dinner the candles threw shadows ten feet high on to the walls. Aunt Zita ate without making any sound. A woman from the village brought in a chicken, which my father carved, and a dish of vegetables. I thought of Aunt Zita's feasts in the kitchen long after my mother and father had gone to sleep: the wild boars' heads and the swans, and pastries stuffed with larks and linnets – the magic dishes, Chinese boxes of dough, each tiny house revealing another smaller, down to the plaited sugar nest of the humming-bird, the currant eye of the white sugar pike. The kitchen had been draped with cloth, and there were candlesticks of golden stags, and gold bowls to drink from, with cinnamon in the hot wine. Aunt Zita wore a fiery dress then, where the flames crawled over the stiff gold skirt, always trying to climb up to the bodice encrusted with gold beads, and the pearls, sometimes flushed to a pale rosy glow by the fire, so tight against her neck they seemed to be embedded there. Aunt Zita smiled at my father, but he looked away. He had possibly for one moment looked into Aunt Zita and, like a landscape seen in lightning, glimpsed the feasts where he was no longer invited, and felt fear.

Already, as they ate, groups of his possessions, her old playmates, were arranging themselves in the house in her schemes and patterns: cushions and rocking-horses, books and old riding-saddles and dusty curtains long ago bundled away and replaced by my mother. Some of the rooms, which had seemed boundless to Aunt Zita as a child, were now taking on gigantic proportions and were filling with the animals and several-headed monsters of her early dreams. My mother was no longer in control of her home, of the house she had been told was her home since her marriage to my father. I knew she dreamed of escape, but she saw only the farm above the house, and the blackness of it on a starless night when the mountains rising steeply behind the farm buildings can be taken, with terror, for the sky – and beyond the farm the road ended and there was nothing but the hills to come at her, rearing up, as she drew near, like stone

16

horses. She saw the chicken-run, and the road that went just above it and led out of the valley. But Aunt Zita had left her traces of blue fire there, and my mother would be burned and frozen to death. There was nothing for it but to stay, in the dining-room which already had turned sympathetically to Aunt Zita, and to live like a prisoner in the shifting ruins of her home.

'Will you go to Hastings this year?' my father asked Aunt Zita. They had eaten tinned fruit and cream, and she smiled still, her flames having already consumed the boring meal and her insatiable appetite for excitement shining out of her eyes.

'Hastings?' said Aunt Zita. 'Doesn't it seem a long way away?'

I knew what she meant, although my mother looked at her almost malevolently when she spoke, as if this new whimsicality was too much to suffer. The blue, ruled bays of the south coast, where Aunt Zita sometimes stayed with 'old friends', were as far as the Pacific from the rough night outside, and the rocks and the trees.

'No, I don't think I'll go,' said Aunt Zita.

My mother rose, to show the meal was over. We followed her through the hall, where paraffin lamps had been put on the tables: the trouble at the dynamo was presumably serious. The sitting-room, lit only by candles, gave off all the tedium of the long evenings of the nineteenth century. Caught in their unchanging lives, the daughters of the house played the piano, and coughed, and read poetry aloud in dying voices. Nothing could ever happen to them. Boredom tapped at the window, like a branch, and the sons of the house filled up glasses of brandy and threw down the King of Hearts on to the floor before grinding their heels into his face. My father's grandmother, in a puckered cap, smiled serenely on her quarrelsome brood, for she had made her suffering into martyrdom. And besides, there was the food to plan every day, and that was perishable: she moved about the house with the ease, with the predictability, of the seasons.

My mother looked around the room, and in turn, a habit she had had many opportunities to imitate, she puckered her lips and assumed a saintly expression. These people – whom even my father must have sensed vaguely, because he moved restlessly in his chair and kept looking over his shoulder, throwing his head back as if he had heard a murmur, came only when it was time to welcome Aunt Zita. But my mother knew them well enough by now. In her way, she could be as strong in her martyrdom, and her sense of virtue, as Aunt Zita with her wilfulness and her fire. My mother took up her sewing. This always infuriated Aunt Zita, who was made nervous by the numbers of pale, unresisting women in the room, and who wanted my mother to talk to her, to prostrate herself before her greater power. Aunt Zita rose to go to bed. She had only one trick to play now – and my mother knew it. There was a pause between them while the piano played a dismal tune, and Aunt Zita's dead grandmother's needle went in and out of the petit-point with a sound like escaping sighs.

'But even though I'm not going to Hastings I shall leave here on the usual date,' said Aunt Zita.

My mother looked up at last, and at that moment the lights came on. The candles seemed to have no brightness in them at all, and Aunt Zita's fire became invisible, so that her startlingly pale face and white dress made her ghostly. My father looked at her in sudden anguish and once more looked away.

'It's entirely up to you,' said my mother. But her sense of relief gave pale red spots of colour to her cheeks. The smile of martyrdom disappeared, then resurrected itself as she

18

remembered that this was still only the first day of Aunt Zita's visit. She sewed on, stabbing the faded wool flowers with blunted fingers.

Aunt Zita went up to bed after some charming farewells. She had been kind to put my mother's mind at rest. But the house was disturbed still at her coming. The rain and wind beat on the windows. The timbers of the house creaked like an old ship. Aunt Zita went smiling to her room, the front room she hated where there was never any sun.

Sometimes Aunt Zita, instead of feasting down in the big kitchen after my parents were asleep, decided to go further afield: then, knowing by the faint movements on the top floor of the house that the maids were getting her ready, I got ready too: an old evening dress of my mother's from the cupboard in the passage, and shoes from before the war, with straps at the ankles. The dress was green, and faded in patches. An artificial rose dropped from the front, like a flag. The dress was stiff, from hanging up so long, and it seemed to force me down the dark corridor past my parents' room, and to walk me up the skeletal, curved staircase to the hushed, higher part of the house. Uncle Ralph's clocks and analysis engines ticked from behind closed doors as I went. He might have been sleeping, or he might have been deep in one of his biological experiments where he slept for a week on end and then not at all for a month, keeping his eyes propped open until the lights in his sight went out. Often he wouldn't greet Aunt Zita at all, until her visit was nearly over. He feared the effect she could have on his machines, with her casual, wonderful powers, and he had run from her room once, along the landing where my father's strange relations were housed by my mother, in terror at her methods. Meals were taken up to him in these periods, and the food was likely to be found untouched outside the door after several days. Uncle Ralph said Aunt Zita had turned it into frogs when he had taken it in, and he had had to throw it out again. Of all things, Uncle Ralph most hated metamorphosis. He believed only in science – so did my father – and the two of them would spend days on end in Uncle Ralph's ticking room.

On those evenings when Aunt Zita was going out, the north wind waited outside her window, as fat as a full pillowcase, a broad, icy back which would take her to every country, to every ball and café, to anywhere she could stave off her boredom. The maids pulled at her stays, and by the time she turned in her room at the sound of me coming in, she was so small round the waist that that part of her body might have been removed altogether, the wind and starless night blowing in there and leaving her a floating head and shoulders, and a wide, black skirt. Her eyes were glittering. She was putting droplets of jet in her ears. The fire round her was damped down, and the maids were sighing and smiling, for you could still feel the heat from her but it was under control. One of the maids had pins in her mouth. Aunt Zita's hem was being taken up a little – and an arched foot leaped out from under the black taffeta frills. The wind outside moaned and leaned against the house. I thought of my parents stirring on the floor below, dreaming of the timbers of the roof going up into the sky, or the walls subsiding under the vast muscle of the wind. Aunt Zita felt them too, and her foot went to the ground in a stamp of impatience. She had no desire to be found by them, and nor had I, in my mother's old dress and the sandals that had many years ago glided obediently with my father over polished floors.

Aunt Zita asked me where I would like to go, but it was only a formality. She knew the world: I knew the village at the top of the garden, I knew the chicken-run, and I knew the road that led from the village, and was sometimes impassable but which was the only way out of the valley. I knew a map of the world, in the one building that was apart from the village, and that was the school. There Maurice and I stared at the map, covered in inkspots, on the wall above the small bookcase. The teacher had lived in the school with her husband, and then he had died. There were marks of tea on the wall above the map, where she had thrown her cup at him. There were trees all round the school-house and the view of the valley was poor. Beneath the garden, and the sloping playground, cemented at the beginning of the war, was a buried village, eight hundred years old, in humps under the trees.

'Shall we go to the ball?' said Aunt Zita. When she said this, her room began to fill with the people who always came with us on these occasions – and I knew she was in her most excited mood, at her most determined to pull back the past, to string herself with light, and sparkling goblets, and the fire festivals where she used to dance.

The people who were coming into the room would have astonished my parents. They looked as if they had walked out of paintings, or as if they must have come from some ancient royal court, because their robes were rich and studded with pearls. Aunt Zita was always worldly: she had no sympathy with the times in which we lived, and she would gladly have sold the village at the top of the garden into bondage for one more jewel, or for a different novelty at her nightly ball. Soon she was surrounded by her troupe. The two midgets in turbans were merchants, and they pulled stones from the silk swathed round their heads. Aunt Zita chose a yellow diamond, which they told her would glint like the sun. Aunt Zita was satisfied, and slipped it on to her finger. There was a woman with feathers on her head dyed to the same false, ugly colour as Maurice's willow-herb and she, like a circus ringleader, was the one who drew

Aunt Zita aside, in the direction of the window, and showed her the north wind, chafing just below, saddled and thick with mist it was impatient to throw off. We all followed then – the women with cameo faces and ringlets and the men in coats of shining brocade. The woman with the feather head-dress opened the window, and we heard the wind howling outside for us.

Sometimes it seemed that we'd never be able to get out of the narrow valley. The hills were steep, and although it was too dark to see them they seemed to be pressing in on us, piled up against the night. Their flanks of quarried stone were where we might end, half-buried. The wind always shrieked as we rose above the house and headed for the ravine, and the cleuchs filled with heather that burned grey in strips in winter. We lurched and tossed, like the flying machines Uncle Ralph constructed and sometimes let loose from his windows. Aunt Zita held me as we passed over the village. We never looked behind us, at the house where the ghostly maids had put out their phantom lights, and which, if it had been seen from an aeroplane high above, would have appeared only as a great shadow, it was so deep in the surrounding valley. We looked down at the village. The ten houses known as The Street, where the farm workers lived, was a grey arm jutting out from the farm buildings. The first frost, brought by Aunt Zita and the north wind, had whitened the fields. On the roof of Peg's shop were two squares of white tiles, like new windows. The road down from the farm, and past Peg's shop to the school, was in blackness. The school itself was a lump, and could have been part of the low, thick wood which grew all round it, blocking the view even of the small ornamental stretch of water at the bottom of the hill beneath the building, and the ruins of the ancient village. Only the cement playground gave a whitish glow, from the frost and the faint starlight.

Peg's shop was visited by my mother and Aunt Zita every time she came, on the day after her arrival and every day after that, as if the transaction of handing money over to someone else might free them from the guilt they felt at the evil thoughts they had about each other. They stood in the shop, visible to Peg only from the waist up, on the far side of the wooden counter scratched with penknife blades: my mother was in a woollen cap that always came out to mark the end of the summer and the arrival of Aunt Zita, and Aunt Zita in one of her extraordinary hats, part felt and part feather, which swept the ceiling the colour of tea from the cigarette Peg never let go. They on the other hand could see the whole of Peg, as she moved about in the ramshackle shop, searching in shoeboxes for the things they claimed to want. They could see her tiny body, in long grey skirt and grey wrapover cardigan, and her gingery head as it popped up, features confused, among the unsaleable goods. She was never sure if their long wait for an item – a pencil with a rubber on the end, an orange book of stamps, a bottle of ginger beer – was maddening to them, or whether it was part of the ritual. These great women, whose bodies could for all she knew have ended in mermaids' tails beneath the counter – or be welded together, like fairground monsters – were for a time at one in the presence of Peg. She was serving them together, she was holding up their walk on the land where there was nothing to buy, only the rows of trees planted by Aunt Zita's grandfather to look at, or the old kitchen garden which my mother had 'let go' because of the war; she was filling in their morning. My mother always took a scrumpled pound note from a leather purse in her pocket, although she could just as well have put anything on account: my father owned the shop. Aunt Zita had a shoulder bag, which I envied – she carried it everywhere, even on visits to the farm. It had powder and lipstick inside, and a smell that reminded me of our magic trips—scent, and a slightly burning smell, like the flares of white fire outside the magnificent houses where she danced all night. She brought out shillings and florins, all new and shining. Peg scooped them into a tin box and gave muddy pennies in change. I felt she liked Aunt Zita's new money, and liked Aunt Zita for it, as if Aunt Zita had somehow manufactured it herself, while she despised my mother's note.

Peg always stayed in the shop, in the little sitting-room next to it or in the bedroom upstairs, week in and week out and from one year's end to the next. My mother thought it strange that she never went to the nearest small town, eight miles away—but she stayed in the shop, and the food vans that came to the village were enough for her, and she had no living relations that anyone knew. Because of this, she and the shop came to look more and more alike: even the air in the shop, which was as fusty and gingery as Peg's whispery bun of hair, seemed to be part of her. Ginger striped cats lay in the old sweet boxes. The lemonade in dusty bottles turned a dull yellow. Toffees as dim as the inside of the shop slid from their jars with a crackling sound on to Peg's dry palms. Because people paid Peg for her goods, and paid her for them in real money, and could even buy real stamps there which would send their news to the outside world, she escaped being considered a witch.

The first ball of the season, as Aunt Zita put it, was always rather a disappointment. I had looked forward to it so long —and had suffered my mother's suspicious, disapproving looks, and the transformation of the house, and a feeling of stiffness in the village so that people going into Peg's shop seemed to examine the sweets with special attention, as if expecting an ordinary stick of rock to turn into a broom-stick and carry them when they weren't looking into another world. Perhaps the sudden end of summer brought on the sense of being let down. My father tapped the barometer every day, and the needle swung to Stormy. Aunt Zita stood beside him, and her face was reflected in the glass, with the needle swinging between her eyes. Leaves began to blow into rooms that were never used, and then scattered in packs when a door was opened. At night, before going to bed, my father went round the house trying to catch them, and I heard him trudging about, long after he was supposed to be asleep, running at the leaves and swearing. Sometimes I followed him secretly. And sometimes I saw that the leaves had taken on the shape of rats, with exquisitely stitched waistcoats in gold and dull red, each seam as fine as a spider's thread. They had bright eyes, which flickered in the dark. I saw their shadows as they ran along the landings, and the ludicrous, bobbing shadow of my father as he panted along the wall with a broom. Some blew up the curved stairway and lay in bales of soft and faded silk at the feet of the ephemeral maids. Russet browns and a dim yellow the colour of the mushrooms that grow in beech woods, and the grey of bark-moss were velvets and chiffons that tore and fell into rivulets and then went into nothing at the touch of a hand.

On the upper landing, where Uncle Ralph resisted the equinoctial changes brought by his sister by cowering in his room and refusing to come out to see the flying leaves and rich stuffs spread over the banisters, they turned to bats like little flying rats, with velvety grey capes on their backs. While my father rushed after them, and the broom swirled over his head, they flew at high speed into the pictures my mother had banished up there: the huge, awkward painting of Aunt Zita as a child, with black ringlets and unfinished hands, and her father and her aunts in the background – and the interiors of cathedrals in bright unfaded paint, and the banks of dull rivers the colour of mustard. The bats made no sound, but some of them dived into the pictures and disappeared. In the morning, when my father hunted for them again with brush and pan, they could be seen in the corners of the paintings – leaves like scraps of torn cloth on the floor at Aunt Zita's feet, aisles and pews of the cathedrals choked with them, as if the roof had blown off and they had settled in the ruin. Uncle Ralph, on his way over the hard green cord carpet to the bathroom, refused to look to left or right. My father, although he was so anxious to catch the leaves, never saw the ones that had been caught between frame and glass. By the end of the autumn they had always melted away. But for days after Aunt Zita came, the bodies of bats were found in the garden, or on the tiled floors down by the kitchen. My mother refused to acknowledge them. By then their capes were faded and torn, and most of the autumnal brilliance had gone. They were buried by my father, in the rubbish heap down by the chicken-run.

The nights of hunting for the leaves were the worst for Aunt Zita because she couldn't get away to the ball. If my father had seen her he would have stopped her from going. Yet when we did go, for the first time at least, there was something so formal, and so expected, about the whole thing that I never enjoyed myself. I thought of the valley we had left, and the forest of old trees on the side of the hill facing the house, where I had seen my mother watch Aunt Zita as she went through some of her transformations in the grassy clearing near the top of the wood. My mother had looked sulky and resigned, as if promising herself she would never let Aunt Zita's tricks impress her. Most of the time she walked alone, on a path of new leaves the sudden wind had torn from the trees, and Aunt Zita flapped among

26

the branches over her head, as a blue jay or a kingfisher. Sometimes a fox darted across my mother's path. Then occasionally Aunt Zita would turn up again, in the old fur her mother had left in the box-room on the upper landing, and they would walk together as if nothing had happened. Aunt Zita had gone off probably to look for a rare plant among the birches. My mother carried a stick on these walks. She might have thought that Aunt Zita would come at her in the shape of a bear, or that a tree would crash against her path just one second away from killing her. My father was never told about these disappearances, and the tame birds and hares with wide eyes which replaced Aunt Zita on the conventional walks about his land. He would have laughed. My mother kept her lips pursed, and always came back with a scarf-ful of bright red and white spotted mushrooms, and chunks of yellow fungus that had been lying like a second leg along the trunk of a tree.

We were never back from the ball until dawn. It took so long to leave the mountains and fly through the mist to the kingdom where Aunt Zita was perpetually served by smiling footmen. In this other time, which seemed to float beside the one my mother and father lived, we might have arrived in any country. Aunt Zita said from time to time that we were in Portugal, or France, or a French Caribbean island like Guadeloupe. The temperature never affected us. And the house where the ball was given was always the same: a grey stone building, classical, with pillars and a portico and flares of fire in bronze torches which we could see miles beneath us before we came down. In the gardens were follies and the ruins of temples and a wild glade where Aunt Zita could summon up the fire spirits if she felt in the mood. The music was very polite and formal, too – and Aunt Zita never went to the glade on the first night, so we danced with the courtiers who had come in our train, and stood in front of tall, ornate mirrors which threw our faces back at us, and we yawned behind our fans. Aunt Zita was interested in seeing if any new games of power had taken place since last autumn. Sometimes an eldest son had been killed in a duel, or a wife had eloped with a lover and a whole estate gone to ruin, but they seemed unchanging to me, so it was a mystery that I looked forward to the first ball so much, and even expected something new to happen at it.

On the days after our evening flights it was my mother who looked pale and haggard, as if she had poisoned herself with thoughts about us. In the middle of her cheeks were pin-points of scarlet and a dank breath came out of her. She was as viciously and unexpectedly coloured as the red and white mushrooms she gathered under the birches. In her fury at Aunt Zita's freedom, at the transformed landscape, hills like the chins of malign gods, plants grouped in sympathies, hedges of Elizabethan box which had sprung up around them, sunken gardens and brick paths laid out in a forgotten set of cabbalistic twists and turns – in hatred at the herbs, the silver-grey of the rosemary, which went from grey to green and back to silver as soft and bright as the head of a moth, all with the speed of the shifting shutters of memory – in rage at the samphire, the comfrey, the roses that had been made like painted faces – my mother produced all the confinements and refinements of her own restricted age. Even before breakfast, while Aunt Zita still lay in bed resting, and the endless crackle and rustle, like the sound of distant fire, came down to us from her ghostly maids, things were rearranged in the house and traps were set. My father sat with his tea in the study on such days. He knew, probably, that he would have to come out with a thunderbolt and disperse the whole house and the valley, smash them to smithereens, before my mother and Aunt

Zita would fall quiet. But he had no energy for the scene, of course, and no desire to upset his sister. He must have thought, as he watched the first cold rain of the end of the year go past his study window, that he had had enough of his family. Yet his family – now that my mother's frail hold on his house was gone – was just what she insisted on giving him. He became agitated, and went in and out of the study too often, so that the door seemed to snap open and shut behind him like a steel spring.

My father's mother was there, and all the daughters too, and by the time Aunt Zita was halfway down the stairs there was a great ceremony in the hall. My mother had clothed the legs of a piano in frilled knickerbockers. There were bouquets of white flowers, sickeningly sweet in smell, mementoes of the calm days of the long summer, before the grass turned yellow, days when the small stone houses in the village each had a door open on to the back garden and women pushed aside washing to walk to the food van, or the travelling library from the town. There was a font at the end of the hall – and the hall had grown even taller, and had sucked in its windows to a religious shape, giving the whole area the appearance of a Victorian church; and there was a minister holding a child, in robes as stiff and papery-white as the scented flowers. Was the child already dead? Its head fell back too softly. Or was it Aunt Zita, in this complicated game my mother was playing with her sister-in-law? Was she showing my father the birth of the bone of contention between them?

On these occasions my father's mother never saw me, nor did her consumptive daughters, and I felt that from the grave their disapproval washed over my mother and myself, as if something was the matter with our bones, some sinew lacking which made our faces and our jaws misshapen. They all, like Aunt Zita, had brows of marble, noses drawn at a school of Fine Art, necks and shoulders so perfectly balanced to their heads that seeing them stand together was to find oneself caught in a colonnade. Our blood was weaker than theirs, diluted: and it was possible to believe that my father had had no connection with us at all, but had been bound a long time, always faithful, in an Egyptian alliance with his sister. Even at these family gatherings, where he darted in and out of his study before my mother caught him and held him firm in place, he seemed to belong absolutely with them, and to be of another species from my mother and myself. His family looked balefully at my mother – she was brave to perform in this way, but her desire for revenge was stronger than caution – and in the shafts of light the colour of dark gold that came in through the stained glass there were glances which fluttered away from the sight of us, the miscegenation, the *mariage morganatique*, the links that would be the first to break in the chain.

Aunt Zita was certainly disturbed by having her family handed to her like this. The horrible limitations of her childhood returned to her, and she squirmed on the hard bench, narrow as a coffin lid, under the family coat of arms. Her eyes turned to the window, but the hills and the wind lashing at the larches, the wind that would always carry her away from us, were obscured by the rich, false colours of piety. Aunt Maddie and Aunt Lucy's faces were in the window, yellow curls and white faces, chaste, swooning in suppressed desire in the mock medieval castle of their dragon father. Chinks of blue glass made their eyes. They were as enclosed as Aunt Zita now, but envying her journeys to the end of the earth they looked at her without love or understanding.

My mother enjoyed these scenes almost too much. She made me sit with her, at the front of the church and in full view of the family pew, and she turned constantly to watch the expression of suffering on Aunt Zita's face. Some of the village people sat next to us – not Peg, who would never go inside a church, nor Maurice, who scuffed his heels outside until I came to play with him – but Willie, who worked on the farm, and his wife Minnie. Willie's hands were broad and rough, and covered his face entirely when he prayed. Minnie had a smell of apples. They were better to look at than my father's family, who, having put out Aunt Zita's fire, by now were stiff and identical, like a set of plaster casts of classical statues left for some malicious purpose in a church. Willie's legs were bowed from sitting on a tractor. Minnie, who dusted in the house each week, competing at this time of year with Aunt Zita's maids but normally quiet, slightly humming as she went around the rooms, was thin, with grey hair in a bun – and she seemed, sitting there under the eyes of the minister, to have felt she must rejoice or sorrow at every one of my father's family occasions.

I recognised that it was my father's brother who was being baptised. This was one of my mother's cruellest punishments, and I saw she didn't dare turn to look at my father as the ceremony went on. Only despair at Aunt Zita's power, and the unfamiliar house which had arranged itself to suit Aunt Zita and my father, with cupboards suddenly locked and refusing to open to my mother's key, and concealed rooms in the highest turrets where their childish laughter shrieked and moaned all day in the wind ... and my mother chasing upstairs after them, to find bedrooms empty and cold and smelling of mothballs when only a moment before she had heard them scuffling in there ... and Uncle Ralph's silence, in the room under the boar's head, with the black bristle of its crown going white in a parting, like the Beast who suffered so long for Beauty ... all this had driven her to perform the most powerful of her tricks. It was also a declaration of enmity. The whole family had to be present, and the colours had to be strong in the church—a late summer sun outside coming in through the crowned saints and the blood of the Lord and falling in ruby tears on the faces of my father's family. Blue stones danced across the cheeks of his dying aunts, who appeared, in the tall pew that was also shot with scudding colour, ridiculous and pathetic, like mummers in an ancient play. The tragedy of the family was being re-enacted before their eyes. I wondered how my mother had the strength to do it—she must have studied the subject, in all the long afternoons when Aunt Zita and my father had gone to visit the farm, or walked over the hills without her. She had come across the faded photographs perhaps, of the baby in white lace, and the little boy on his mother's knee, maternal eyes flashing and the child too securely anchored, so that his first flight from her would inevitably end in death. She had gone, when she was abandoned in the house, and even the summer had gone, rain as thin and green as the paint in the old rooms falling drearily at the windows—and Uncle Ralph pacing beside his machines or closed in some cupboard, hanging like a great bat upside down in the darkness, proving a new biological clock—she had been led to the small room by the disused nurseries, where a Victorian bath was boxed in by the wall and a picture of my father's brother's earliest club was hanging from a pin. She must have stared a long time at the six sitters, in their boaters and striped ties. My father's brother, at that point, had two months to live. Above him and his friends a tall skylight went up in the bathroom ceiling and far from reaching the sky was extinguished in an attic, so that the light which came down from above was dark green and filtered, and the forgotten shrine seemed to have been submerged in water. My father's mother would never have allowed such a relic to end up there. It must have been Aunt Zita, who was afraid to see the face of her long-dead brother, who had hung it up, casually knocking in a pin. I don't think my father ever noticed it. But my mother would go suddenly to that part of the house, where the children had been brought up – it was the only part of the house Aunt Zita didn't change – and come back refreshed.

The minister named the child. My father's family still sat like the dead in the back pew. It was strange the baby's mother didn't hold him, and that there were no godparents, but the ritual my mother was forcing them to witness was gone through like this to underline the child's doom, its death before its twentieth year: to show them how unhappy they would feel when he had gone: to remind my father and Aunt Zita how different their lives would have been if he had lived.

Indeed they would have been. The child was the eldest. My father would have had to go away, to live miles distant from his youth. My mother wouldn't have had to live where she did – and there would have been no visits from Aunt Zita. The child was to grow into a strong character, who killed his sister's jealousy with scorn. Had he lived she would scarcely have come to her old home, to bend the walls and contort the valleys and gain her freedom again and again on the back of the north wind. As they watched, and the infant gave a feeble scream at the first splash of cold water, they saw the difference its survival would have made to all of them. At this moment, my mother too saw the difference – and as she stared at the almost-invisible face of the child, a whole lifetime of another life, in another house with a man who was my father but also another man from my father, ran out in front of her like smoke and filled the church. I had to hold her, as she became restless at my side. Willie and Minnie looked away from her. When the bubble burst, and she found herself alone, crossing the hall towards my father's study to tell him that lunch was ready, I ran behind her and clung on to her arm. She always looked down at me, and caught my eye, and smiled.

My mother's trick, however, was frequently turned against her by Aunt Zita. Once summoned, the long-dead relations never entirely went away, and after her first anguish at coming up against the past, Aunt Zita would introduce them and laugh in triumph at my mother's confusion. On our walks, which were circular, monotonous and named after the days of the week so that the inevitability of their recurrence hung heavy from one week's end to the next, they would appear like the grotesque, revolving figures on a clock: sometimes naked, my father's elder brother and three muscular, straw-boatered friends playing early morning tennis on the disused tennis court; sometimes in bright dresses with bright plaid shawls, coughing daughters taking the damp air in the hills. My mother always turned pale when she saw them, and twisted her hand round the handkerchief she kept with her all the length of Aunt Zita's visit, and her hand became a round ball. Aunt Zita sometimes spoke to her relatives. Polite words and laughter were exchanged. At these times Aunt Zita's fire burned low, and there was a crushing quietness in the air, which was difficult to breathe, as if it had been dumped in the valley by the mountains, and was being held down by them. Clouds of midges, which came in the warm spell after Aunt Zita's abrupt autumn, made floating heads beside the talkers. Yet the strange part was that despite the quietness I could never understand what they were saying. In these lost conversations with the dead, the vowels and inflections were far away and incomprehensible. Did my mother understand? More than I did, I thought—but I never liked to ask her. We would all stand sometimes, by the corner of the farm steading, for as much as ten minutes while Aunt Zita chatted with her family. To the right of us were the byres, and The Street where the farm workers lived, and if we were to follow it we would be enmeshed in the Tuesday walk, along the side of the steepest mountain. If we turned to the left, parallel lines of melancholy firs would lead us into the depths of the valley, into the deepest corner of the cup, which held a small lake scattered with islands. I looked up at the hill, and wondered if we would go for the Tuesday walk. Already the mists were coming down, first in thin furls separated by purple strips of heather, so that the base of the mountain seemed to be detached from the ground and to have become a great tapestry, a menacing wall-hanging striped with flares of dim purple. Beyond this un-certain fabric was the land where Aunt Zita's family lived. I thought of her elder brother going back there, with his adoring mother on his arm. It was cold there, and the mist went straight into the lungs. On the days Aunt Zita trapped us at the crossroads, the muddy intersection by the farm buildings, and kept us waiting as she flirted with her elder brother, I prayed that we would go to the left, follow the valley to its natural end, slap up against the lake and the ravine. I shrank from Aunt Zita's tricks, and swore I would never humour her again.

After the first week of Aunt Zita's visit, the blue shadows left the corners of the house and the north wind lay quiet behind the hills. My father stopped rubbing his nose, and stood instead at his study window staring up at the sky. An Indian summer had come. But it was like a woman with skirts cut off up to the knee – startled and unsure. The mornings and early evenings were white and cold, ragged, where the real, long summer had been as round and full in each day as the first navigator's picturing of the globe. The flowers in my mother's herbaceous borders had been nipped once, and made little response to the false sun.

The petals of the white flowers were as dry as paper. Only I was every year deluded, and went to fetch my dog from Willie and Minnie's, down the hill (Aunt Zita wouldn't have a dog in the house); for that week, which was no more than a chink in the fortifications of winter, I thought that everything had become all right again, and we ran on the grassy path as if the frosts hadn't seized the yellow, scythed grass and turned it as sere as an old man's tea-stained moustaches.

In that week, as if deluded too by the artificial season, the landscape turned back to normal again. Aunt Zita's fire was very low, her first impact had gone, and she sulked in the simulacrum of the beautiful days which had preceded her coming. The quarried side of the mountain which faced the east of the house no longer had the stamp of her features in the slate jutting of her jaw, or the mossy overhang of her dark hair. Her arms no longer lay along the top ridges of the mountains, white as marsh mist, resting nonchalantly on cloudberries and pools of peat water. The correspondences, too, were gone: the greenhouse, a lurking monster when my mother went to see if the apricots were ripe, became a simple house of glass. In the derelict old forest, where fungus was demolishing the trees and where in her first week Aunt Zita flapped as a bright jay or trotted with a fox stink along the path just ahead of my mother, no changes or conversions took place. The return of summer showed the three-legged stool as a raft of bracken and prickly bush. In the half-fallen glades, where the souls of changed people wandered and rested in portals of shadow and rotting bark, there were only the signs of the frost's first attack: toadstools bitten at the edges, lichen on the birch trunk that looked as if it had been sprayed with a deadly gas. My mother took advantage of this week of respite to revisit the places she had always been most drawn to. It was pathetic to watch her pleasure at their recovery. We started the walks in that period, and came back for lunch later every day, with my mother beaming with health, and Aunt Zita, even if she had conjured her brother and her mother and her delicate sisters, pale and suffering from their infectious cough. It was enough for my mother to see the house obedient to her once more, for the rooms to have returned to the functions which my mother had allotted them, for the views on to the gardens to lack the herbalists' symmetry and to show her ordinary, colourful borders, for her to glow all the more with restored confidence. In these days Aunt Zita smoked a lot, and crushed the stubs at the lunch table into a crystal container near my father's plate. I saw him for the first time look at her in distaste. Her lighter was gold and tubular, but it was clear, as she lifted it to the tip of a cigarette, that she was the one who supplied its fire. My mother, who didn't smoke, was able at last to exchange glances the length of the table with my father. He looked back at her gravely as the smoke rose over his food and banked about three feet above his head, before drifting to the edges of the room.

In these ordinary days Aunt Zita went often to the old nurseries, as if trying to exorcise the power of her family in the surroundings where she had been most helpless and dependent on them. I followed her there, in the long passages, leaving my exultant mother alone with my father, and feeling for Aunt Zita as I always did, in her icy loneliness. She was small, smaller than my mother, and she went on these pilgrimages with a straight back and a high head. The house, no longer under her control, seemed only grudgingly to let her pass, and the dim prints of ambitious, hatted women had averted eyes. If Aunt Zita failed to find her power again, she would have to leave, to terminate her visit: a scandal, a triumph for my mother which she could never survive. Every year, in the white, fallow week that lay between her arrival and the first winter storms, it seemed that she would never recover herself. The whispering maids on the upper floor were silent. Uncle Ralph, aware immediately of the decline of her influence, came down to meals and brought with him butterflies and moths pinned on thin wood, long lists of new words for the ideal language he was inventing, and trays of the jumbled innards of Swiss watches, which coiled and slithered like caterpillars, and once caught between his agile fingers were turned to engine a miniature car or a talking manikin.

'Ralph, where are you living now?' Aunt Zita would ask.

My mother looked trapped at this, and stared anxiously at the knives and forks beside her place, as if they were imprisoning her.

'Still in Malmesbury?' Aunt Zita pressed. It seemed unfair indeed that my father's brother should be allowed to stay the year long in the turrets of his childhood while she, doomed to roam the world for husbands, excitement, fire, was rationed to three weeks. My father looked at her over his steaming plate. Since there were no more banquets in the gold-festooned kitchen after hours, and the shrieking of the north wind seemed as if it had never been, the shepherd's pies and stews normally consumed had taken on the appearance of perfectly acceptable food. I heard Aunt Zita sigh. Without her aides she was impotent. The party-going crowd, courtiers, dwarfs, turbaned merchants, no longer came to her room in the night. Her yellow diamond, confronted with the real sun that came in through the dining-room windows, looked like a drying patch of yellow water. And her own skin, the marble whiteness fed by fire, was as faded as silk.

'You know I sold the house in Malmesbury to Wilhelmina a long time ago,' said Uncle Ralph calmly.

'So where are you living, then?' demanded Aunt Zita.

My mother rose to her feet. The prison had become unbearable to her. On the heated plate on the serving-table lay a log of suet bathed in golden syrup. She gestured to it vaguely. 'Zita, dear, won't you ... '

'I thought you said you were going to buy a flat in London,' Aunt Zita said to Uncle Ralph.

'They were much too expensive,' Uncle Ralph replied.

As the suet was eaten, my father, head down in his commanding chair, would spread his fingers on the table and drum there, as if this inner rhythm would shortly take possession of him and march him away to his study. But he was conciliating; he wanted to include Aunt Zita and Uncle Ralph in a summer afternoon as long and innocent as the summer afternoons of the early years of the century, and despite the impossibility of this he suggested the lake, a picnic, a drive out of the valley into the alien country beyond. My mother, knowing that all these outings would be refused, stared into the pictures that hung round the room. Men with vegetable heads, carrot noses, a succession of horticultural Roman Emperors, were arranged on the walls above the flesh-eaters. But their appeal, which was of the age of sympathies and glimpsed affinities, was gone in this white, opaque week of the loss of Aunt Zita's magic. And the heads appeared an affected concept: my mother had never liked them.

When the meal was over, and Aunt Zita was smoking, Uncle Ralph agreed to go to the lake for an afternoon picnic. My mother, of course, would have to go with them – to take the sandwiches from the basket, to rest the scalding kettle on the damp outdoor fire. She accepted her fate, although Aunt Zita would be left the house, and might cruelly have transformed it by the time she returned. She glanced at me, in the hope I would go to the lake with them. I stayed with Aunt Zita.

Aunt Zita walked at speed to the nurseries, once the car had left the front of the house, and my mother, staring apprehensively at the sky for a sign of a break in the weather, a portent of the return of the north wind, was no longer visible, a white scarf tied over a straw hat in the seat at my father's side. Aunt Zita, in her narrow boots, took on the whole enmity and indifference of the house, and if it seemed that the walls might lean in on her and suffocate her she went all the faster, to elude their toppling embrace. In the heart of the house there was none of the summer that dallied outside. It was dark, and slightly warm. There was a smell of mothballs, and an irregularity in the worn brown carpets, as if moles tunnelled and had thrown up hills. After the glare of the hall, and the bright departure to the lake, the women in the prints were hardly visible – a blur of a hat, like my mother's tied under the chin with a gauze scarf—sourly disapproving of Aunt Zita's aims.

It would be clear to anyone that Aunt Zita was in search of love. She moved with determination, buttocks hardly moving in the long strides her legs accomplished, her walk seeming to hold in fire which might otherwise fall from her and be wasted. In my ignorance of love, I watched Aunt Zita in the afternoons of her powerless week, falling into ecstasies which seemed to me only part of her magic strangeness. It was odd, certainly, that she was only possessed of this craving when her spirits were low and the world was no longer at her command. And the look in her eyes I was then quite incapable of translating. As she went into her transports of joy, they burned with the adoration of suffering. They pleaded for more pain.

In the old nurseries, which we reached after twisting and turning in corridors as black and airless as Roman streets, there was darkness and absence of calm. The fat yew trees outside the window, once trim and gathered in at head and

40

foot, had stray branches like escaping hair. The branches waved vaguely at the window. In the biggest room, where Aunt Zita's elder brother awaited her embrace, the walls were patterned with trees and berries; plump pigeons sat on the intersecting branches. A faint trickle of soot always seemed to come down this chimney, and it rustled on the shell of white paper in the grate. Above the mantelpiece was a religious scene, in ceramic.

Aunt Zita would stare up at the Madonna in her blue and yellow robes. The Virgin was patting a lamb, which had a green china bow at its neck. The Virgin's face appeared sad, absorbed – and below her, on the mantelpiece, seized by Aunt Zita's eyes, was the photograph of my mother's sister, Aunt Thelma, who was responsible for the scene above. I didn't know how my mother had managed to introduce the photograph, and then permit her sister to put up the pastoral of the Mother of God. Neither belonged to this room, where my father and his brothers and Aunt Zita had been brought up: it was like forcing the offspring of a different animal, in order to deceive the mother, into the true skin.

Aunt Zita was never deceived. She looked into Aunt Thelma's narrow, pious face and then up again at the oval plaque. It grew even darker in the room and she began to sway on her feet. I could feel her desire, but as it was unknown to me I thought instead that I heard the first stirrings of the north wind struggling in the thick centres of the yews, trying to reach the window, to blow away the branches. The soot went down in a steady stream into the grate. Aunt Zita's elder brother stood between the windows, dressed in a flannel blazer and white bags. A pigeon, demoted from its perch by the intrusion of his shoulder, seemed to be standing by his left ear. The bright yew berries on the wallpaper, with their little dabs of white to show transparency, hung from his hair in clusters. An unpleasant whiteness came into the room, like the white light before a storm, and the ceramic lamb gleamed on the wall. Aunt Zita walked towards her elder brother, pulling off her clothes as she went.

Aunt Zita lay on the floor. She was naked, and her skin was white and shining as the lamb that pranced endlessly above her. She opened her legs and began to roll from side to side. I felt Aunt Thelma's silent anger, and a tension that would bring either thunder or the cracking of the Madonna's complacent face, the shattering into powder of her blue and yellow robes. Aunt Zita's elder brother stepped forward. The pigeon and the berries receded from him. He knelt between Aunt Zita's gaping thighs.

Aunt Zita's elder brother had an intelligent, well-meaning face. Before his death he had played the piano in the long room downstairs which my mother had closed and which my father still secretly longed for. There had been parties, and concerts: Aunt Zita's elder brother had been loved by many people. He had owned one of the first small planes (this now belonged to Uncle Ralph) and he had floated above the rim of his land. Once he had crashed into the lake. His friends liked to dress him as an Arab, in those times, and to put him at the head of the table in golden robes and beads. They travelled with him into the desert, on his quests for reassurance, self-abnegation and power. Aunt Zita's elder brother and his friends liked to make up clubs amongst themselves, and to speak in secret languages. The young women they worshipped were as distant as flowers embroidered on a kimono sleeve. If these young women lost their enigmatic quality they were no longer interesting. But with Aunt Zita it was different. She provoked her elder brother's friends. They were ashamed of themselves for falling in love with her so lustily – yet Aunt Zita only loved her elder brother in the end.

The fire rolled out of Aunt Zita in a ball. It lit up her

elder brother's face so that it glowed like the yew berries on the wall behind him, and the yew berries on the branches outside, which were beginning to toss as the fat trees swelled with the wind. His face was white, and glowed under the skin pale red. The small globe of fire, flickering and restless, slid across the floor and lay by the fender, beneath the empty grate. Aunt Zita and her elder brother rocked on the threadbare carpet, which had once carried the same design as the walls and where, rubbed out by the passage of Aunt Zita and her brothers' childish feet, there remained the shadows of pigeons and the lost key of inter-locking branches. Aunt Thelma and the Madonna looked down on them. In the corridors, the women of earlier centuries shifted and creaked in their silk dresses and pinioned hats. It had grown so dark that it was clear there would be a storm. I thought of my mother, and the rain hissing on the damp wood my father and Uncle Ralph had collected, and her apprehensions growing as they went to huddle in the boathouse by the edge of the lake where one room was for human habitation and the other, with a floor of black water, guarded the boat like a monster from the deep.

The fire diminished and went out. It left a pool on the carpet, like an inkspot. It seemed thick, and didn't creep towards Aunt Zita and her elder brother, who now lay without moving in each other's arms.

The rain came, as it always did, from the extreme end of the valley where my mother and father and Uncle Ralph were trying to have their picnic. It was as if the sky had gone down into the cracks in the ravine and the clouds were spewing the rain out from the earth behind the shallow stones. I watched the drops that raced across the window turn to an open fan of water. Aunt Zita slept on. The look of intense joy and suffering had left her face, and she seemed obliterated, as if her elder brother had given her the punishment she craved. Certainly, his sleeping face was self-satisfied, in the faint white glow that came in from the sky.

I met my mother in the hall as she walked in after the abortive picnic. The straw hat and scarf were wet, and her eyes were anxious.

'The weather's broken,' Uncle Ralph said as he came in behind her with the fishing satchel they had packed with food. 'That's the end of the summer, I'm afraid.'

My father closed the hall door. He hummed as he went to his study. He welcomed, I knew, the first storms of winter and the gale-force wind.

On the day before the return to school, the wind slipped back down the chimneys and howled, and the trees began to toss off their leaves so that the grassy path was cluttered with them, and a man in a van came to the house, bringing us trays for inspection: hairpins in packets, brown dog combs, bundles of liquorice allsorts. The trays were partitioned, into wooden lanes that felt sticky at the top. But Aunt Zita liked running her finger down them. She liked the cheap jewellery, and bought a red butterfly with smudged markings. It winked at us from her lapel for the rest of the day.

The growing wind wasn't the only cause for my mother's unease. Since her triumphant afternoon alone in the house, Aunt Zita had produced an effect of stasis, of absolute limbo, where the house seemed destined to waver constantly between the present and the hours of Aunt Zita's youth, in the shadows of autumn lengthening and shortening rooms, bringing down folds of thick curtains, grouping chairs round long-vanished card tables. Electricity, a new invention, flickered blue at the touch of a switch. My father complained of the fast rains and falling leaves blocking the dynamo. He took us all down with him, to the patch of

44

unreclaimed land by the chicken-run. We looked in at the machine that converted the water that swept needlessly from the hills into the valley, and made our dim lights and electric fires. Against its roar came the wind, which rolled over the turrets of the house. The wind gathered in indigo balls of power above the dynamo. I saw Aunt Zita and my father exchange glances, and I knew they no longer knew if they had left childhood. The wind rumbled and collected forces over the dynamo roof. The flimsy glass and asphalt roof looked as if it could be lifted and carried on a single breath over the too-fast-running stream and into the field beyond. Then the machine, turning and thundering, the great engine that kept the house and the valley alight and stationary while the black clouds rolled past, would finally test its strength against the wind, Aunt Zita's harnessed element. The dynamo would grind to a halt, the slowing spokes a grin of defeat. The wind, gathering its huge, ungainly bustle, would make off across the skies with Aunt Zita perched astride the billowing nightclouds. My father and mother would run for Willie to mend the machine before it got too dark to see.

'We need two men from the farm to clear the Hen Pond and then the sluice down here,' said my father.

Uncle Ralph said he would like to clear the Hen Pond. When he had been a child, the pond – above the farm, along a trail on the side of the mountain, had been one day completely emptied. Uncle Ralph remembered the gasping fish, with white bellies that looked as if they were paunches hanging over trousers, and mouths that moved mechanically up and down in search of air, like his own clockwork dolls. There was a surprising amount of litter in the pondweed: old tin boxes, John Player packets, women's bath hats. Uncle Ralph had walked among the dying fish, noting the species. They were all brown trout except for one pike, and he was forced to invent. But he had the list still, the beginnings of his 'museum of possibilities', where speech parts and the vertebrae of prehistoric birds, and unusual collector's pieces, such as the hair of a witch burned by Matthew Hopkins, were laid out and labelled next to his mah-jong set made up of swordfish teeth, and all the other treasures my father unwillingly allowed him to keep in the house. But my father pointed out that the pond would not be dredged today. Only the leaves must be squeezed from the sluice, if the dynamo was to receive the water it needed. Uncle Ralph shook his head, and immediately said he was busy. He wanted no more of leaves, since Aunt Zita's first autumnal shaking of the trees. He had hated the invasion of the bats after the blowing-in of the leaves – and he hated birds, too, which made him distraught when he was down by the chicken-run and heard the chickens whirring up their wings in an attempt to fly. Most of all he feared Aunt Zita's hats, with their monstrous feathers. Sometimes, as she walked up the spiral staircase, intentionally slow, towards his room, a black cockerel, wings at the flap, beak wide open as two fingers in shadow play on the wall, appeared to be craning from her head. Uncle Ralph slammed his door then, and stayed by his classified lists until she was gone.

With the first storms came the first feelings of rebellion, and the village was drawn in tight to itself, the stones on the square grey houses clearly demarcated, as if a child had gone over them in the night with a white pencil, underlining the separateness of each granite slab. The rain poured down, not horizontally but from low clouds always opening and always full. Dark came in now like an unexpected blow before the beginning of a fight, knocking the looming house, and the village and greenhouses above, the chicken-run below and the school half-escaping out of the valley, into an obscurity that wasn't even relieved by stars. And the wind, enormous in the rightness of its time, and refreshed by its rest in the wings while the unimportant scenes were being played, seized and tussled with the gaping clouds, banged them against each other until they groaned, dived through them in eddies which danced the tiles from the roof of the farm buildings, and sent splinters of pure cold along the corridors, reminding Aunt Zita to get her ball-dress ready and her jewels out from their box.

This time, though Aunt Zita couldn't feel it, the resentment was there and growing. In Peg's shop the new issue of stamps had come in, and the people from the village met on the neutrality of her linoleum floor to buy the orange 2/6d booklet and raise their eyes to the heavens at the coming of the wind. They were looking for someone to blame. From Peg's door, which had a glass window as the upper half, they could see the scudding clouds that had already devoured two thirds of the world, for the mountains were gone and even the banks of rhododendron planted between the big house and the village were touched with mist at the top. They saw, too, and were afraid of them before custom blunted the fear, the narrowing months ahead. Peg's cats, eyes already dreamy with winter, perched on the ledge above the counter. The smell of the cats, and their saucer of milk on the floor by the cartons of chocolate bars, and the uneven heat from Peg's electric fire, which, depending on the leaves in the sluice in the Hen Pond, and the power of the wind as it choked the burns with leaves and silenced the dynamo, was either suffocatingly hot as or pale as the stripes on the ginger cats – all these reminded people of their own interiors, and themselves prone in them as prisoners while winter settled in over the hills. They took money for the stamps from their purses and pockets with fingers that ached already with the coming chilblains.

Minnie's rough fingers were sore and red. The cola bottles, and the ginger beer, which people took to the hay-fields and lay sipping in the miraculous, white calm of the long northern summer evenings, were stacked now in the back of the shop. Times were still transitional: the tins of cocoa hadn't yet arrived in the delivery van. But Peg was in her shawl. Flies no longer buzzed in the shop. As the customers went out into the raging air, they shook their heads menacingly.

In the school the teacher was bad-tempered. I sat with Maurice, but our pact of the summer, of the magical old man in the chicken-house, had been blown away by the winds and he sat half-turned from me, as indifferent as Peg's cats, frozen with the boredom of the term that lay ahead. Outside the school the wind fussed in the dark firs the teacher wanted my father to cut down, and blew into the bushes as if they were paper bags. The teacher had been out of the valley for her holidays. She was strained, the pincer grip of the valley had her once, more and the prospect of the lonely winter ahead in the dark shapes of the tossing trees. She punished us for our disobedience and lack of concern by strapping the palms of our hands with a crescent of leather. She looked none of us in the eye as she did this. Yet in the early summer, invited by my mother up for tea at the house, she had made three perfect somersaults – presumably for my instruction – on the circle of grass by the front door.

The map of the world on the wall in the school seemed to have grown even smaller since I had seen Aunt Zita again, and travelled great distances. The large pink continent which was South America suggested that it was on those fat folds – the map had fallen from its drawing-pin so often that the western side of the world was crumpled and dragged up – that I had flown and landed. I thought I could feel the sweet air, and see mournful ruins where Aunt Zita erected her colonial mansion for a night of insolent revelry before going out into the mysterious cities of the Aztecs and making fire in the dawn, as they had done. Islands, no bigger than blobs, lay off the northern coast of the great continent, and I smelt their nutmeg yawn. I knew that tonight, or one night soon, as the wind built its strength and Aunt Zita's blue, fiery lips smiled in greater and greater disdain at my mother, at the dining-room table, at Uncle Ralph's craven absence, we would leave again – and, 'the first ball of the season' over, we would come down in real carnival, in the dream of any dweller in those lonely mountains by the silent lochs.

The teacher called me away from the map. Perhaps she hated the tea stain above it, symbol of a too-restricted life, a domestic squabble hung above the picture of the world. Or perhaps, building her resentment as the others in the village were, she guessed my knowledge of moving through space while they were anchored, and had decided, as Aunt Zita was unavailable to her, to make the most of me as a scapegoat.

In those early days of the rising wind, I walked from school to the house along the back road. The rain had driven deep into the road already, and made puddles Maurice walked through like a giant crossing small seas. The trees were straining to come up by the roots and sail through the air. By the Racket Court, where some of Aunt Zita's old clothes, red velvet dresses and capes, lay in trunks, there was a protective belt of trees. Maurice always ran past them quickly. In the wind they were black and moaning, and their branches rattled. In these days of the rising intolerance of the wind, and the sharp rebellion of the people in the village, one of the trees that guarded the old, discarded treasures of my father and Aunt Zita's family, had been wrenched from the earth and failed to fly. The earth in the wound was surprisingly fresh and brown. The tree lay half across the road, with branches of broken fir rising in semicircles from the trunk, like a crushed centipede. The first day, Maurice tried to jump over it, and the dying, prickly branches pulled feebly at his bare legs. Then we walked the long way round, over the craters in the road and clinging to the fence.

It was a long time since the Racket Court had been used. It looked like a fairly imposing sized house, Swiss perhaps, because it was built of wood and had a cheerful red roof, which had faded in two world wars and the piling years of the century, and had grown a covering of dark green moss, thick as a slipping wig over the tiles. Apart from the black trees by the entrance, it was easy to get in. Many of the children from the village climbed in the broken windows and ran up to the gallery, where once my father's mother had watched her handsome son play indoor tennis with nameless young women from London. The children of thirty years ago, before leaving the valley, going to the mills or south in search of jobs, had prised open the trunks and played in the old clothes. Sets of ivory-backed brushes with Aunt Zita's elder brother's initials half chipped off, and the yellowing bristles too few and soft to brush a head, lay in corners of the Racket Court, as if the children had tried to invent some game in which they could be the pieces.

The velvet of Aunt Zita's red cape was bruised with age and fancy dress games. While the children played grand-mother and the wolf, their parents searched for them and dragged them from the forbidden Racket Court. The property of ghosts, it still wasn't theirs to play in. Dead or alive, my father and Aunt Zita's family owned every branch of every tree, every corner and cupboard in the valley and circling hills.

Once, Uncle Ralph had kept his Percival Gull Six in the Racket Court, and it was possibly because of this that Aunt Zita seldom went down the back road – and if she did, with my mother on the pretext of visiting the two cottages below the school, she never materialised her family there. Aunt Zita, with her own powers to carry her through the air, hated any form of aviation. Uncle Ralph's excitement with goggles and helmet, his slight guilt at being the inheritor from a fallen god of this wonderful machine, and the paraphernalia of string and paper and engine made Aunt Zita's eyes roll with boredom in her head. Even though the Percival Gull was now housed in the stables (another sign of Uncle Ralph's permanence and therefore not mentioned), Aunt Zita walked past the Racket Court as if it had never been built.

On the evening I suspected I would go on the second of my trips with Aunt Zita, Maurice showed me the extent of the growing rage and obstinacy in the village. Because the wind had been hard behind him, prodding him with a thick knuckle and almost knocking him flat as we left the huddles of black trees in the back road and came out by Peg's shop, he turned and dived down the path to the chicken-run. I ran with him. The evening light was sour, and the hen-house and scrappy yard looked desolate in their huddle of corrugated iron roof and dusty glass of the dynamo building squatting to the side of them, all bordered by an overfull burn which went down the side of the garden with a choking sound, and made the grass soggy and treacherous. Maurice picked two reeds that were growing by the side of the burn. He had a small sling. Sometimes we shot the reeds, whittled into arrows, at the old man in the chicken-house. The hens screeched when the reeds went inside the warm, dark house. We were afraid for our eyes as we crawled up the slatted run to see if we had shot the old man, and the hens' beaks and wings came in round us. We slipped on the slatted run spattered with chicken shit, and rolled on the wet grass before we went home, to soak out the stains.

This time, Maurice picked the reeds as before, but he turned his back on the chicken-house and he refused to search for the human turd. He made me walk across the burn, on two logs that rocked a few inches above the brown spate. On the far side, we climbed up through the stiff reeds to the top of the bank. We looked back a moment to get our breath. A half-evening masked the buttresses and crenellations of the house. The light in my father's study was on. In the long drawing-room, which my mother had many years ago condemned to nothingness, two chandeliers shone like sparklers. It was almost possible to see the portraits on the walls – tall women dressed in fading, inferior paint – and the dull parquet. I knew then that Aunt Zita must be preparing herself in the unused room, making the trappings of a ball so that our departure later would go smoothly. I couldn't see her though: only the torch-light flickerings on the upper landing of her returning maids, and the top of my father's head at the desk in his study – squarer than the head of the old man in the chicken-house, but with hair of much the same colour, like the black and white mixed feathers of hens.

Maurice was making me look the other way, away from the house. Behind us, growing up from the compost heap, was his army of willow-herb, which seemed to stretch towards him as he stood on the crest of the bank. Before us lay the fields, and an ornamental pond where Uncle Ralph sometimes practised his new diving equipment, in a depth of four feet, and the bumpy wood which grew over the buried eighth-century village. It was as if the two villages, the old with its position near the entrance to the valley, its strategic height on the mid-slope of a hill – and the new, built by my father's grandfather, were diametrically opposed to each other, in space, in time, in attitudes of dependence and isolation. It was from this buried village, though, that people were walking. From the trees, and mounds of brick that had sunk in a millennium into the leaf mould, and from the skeleton houses, thick with earth, walls strangled by the probing roots of old trees, the people of the village advanced on the house.

Maurice told me to run home. I left him – he didn't hear as I slipped in the burn from the wet logs and fought the brown current to the other bank, nor did he answer when I called to him to come and help me. I went up the garden to the house. I had seen Willie and Minnie in the crowd of advancing villagers, and Minnie's sister Mary who sometimes came to stay, and teased my dog until it bit her. Also Peg, very small and straight in the front row. They could have been armed, but only primitively, like Maurice, and in the dusk it was difficult to see.

Outside the long gallery, where I could see Aunt Zita dancing alone in a fizzle of lights of her own making, the wind slunk, rushed round corners, puffed up at the unnecessary turrets and unfireable stone guns. I went in at one of the garden doors, and immediately saw my mother, as she tramped the long tiled corridor back from a conversation in the kitchen. She was frowning, her face was pale. No doubt, while I had been at school, her day had gone badly with Aunt Zita. And as I was about to warn her of the approaching mob in the fields, I fell silent and went upstairs to get ready for the night.

In the basement, in the long, tiled passages, the white tiles on the walls grew sometimes enormous and sometimes tiny, and in their continuous modulation they shifted like the notes on a piano, silently playing a symphony of rising and falling scale. The red tiles on the floor were dull, however often they were mopped down. Along the tops of the walls were the bells, with the names of the distant superior rooms inscribed beneath them. On excited nights, when the wind was arched under Aunt Zita's window, and the highest floor of the house whispered and giggled, and let off the sound of tiptoeing feet like pistol shots, the bells rang uncertainly in the basement, trilling and then muffled. Aunt Zita pulled at the faded bell-rope in her room when she wanted to summon her maids. The ancient wires carried her message through the interstices of the house, pulsing for a millionth of a second behind the panels of my mother's bedroom, falling from the head of the house to the door of my father's study, so that he looked up vaguely from his desk and peered around, sensing his sister's imperious electricity. When the bells rang, the ghostly maids appeared immediately, as if they had travelled upward through the cumbersome house, along the wires that called them. Aunt Zita would smile, and indicate a dress that needed to be taken from the cupboard. Another maid would take a shoe tree from a black shoe with black ribbons that tied over the instep. Precariously high in the house, they walked lightly in their servants' creaking shoes in front of low windows, while in the basement the bells still shook restlessly from the tugging.

The names of the bells, which were colours and flowers: Heliotrope and Blue, Lavender and Lavender Dressing Room, Miss Zita, Master Ralph, Governess's Room and Campanula, appeared as mysterious announcements on the tiles below. For small wants, for hot water in hip baths taken to the bedrooms, breakfast trays, and for washing still smelling of the steam iron carried in the gloom of the back stairs to the narrow bachelor rooms where friends of my father's elder brother pulled on fresh linen, sweated on

54

the Racket Court and pulled it off again – for these domestic, daily needs the flowery bells rang incessantly. But for trouble, the great bell above the stables sounded out as far as the village, and down as far as the school. A theft in the house might wake its voice, or fire, or a bulletin of war that had just come through the air to make itself heard on the wireless. The sound of the great bell became trapped in the valley, and as the valley contracted in the last mile before falling into a dip of water under the ravine, it hurled itself over the hills and made a dark sound, as thick as a larch wood glimpsed through mist, before it disappeared again. It was seldom used. Yet, on the night when the villagers had been seen at dusk, walking from the village they had never inhabited, it began to ring loudly just as dinner was being served. There were several reasons for this – yet both my father and mother were agitated, and began to wring their hands, and finally ran out into the courtyard, leaving Aunt Zita and me alone.

Sometimes, when the enmity between my mother and Aunt Zita had reached an unbearable pitch, and Aunt Zita's fire was raging unchecked in the house, my father went out silently to the stables. He climbed up the stone stairs past the gunroom where a stuffed black bear stood holding a small tray, and long-pickled adders, pale as tapeworms, lay coiled in jars. He let himself up through a trapdoor, he reached the belfry, and he hung on the rope. As he hung there, calmly rocking, he could see the blaze of the house his grandfather had built, the windows of the hall horribly enlarged by the tearing flames, and the gargoyles, mid-nineteenth-century replicas of forgotten fears, turn livid and spit fire from their contorted lips. The turrets gave off sprays of flame from their conical roofs, and plumes of black smoke which, like the feathers in Aunt Zita's hats, pranced and nodded in the wind. My father always chose a windy night to go and ring the bell – for then, of course, Aunt Zita and my mother were at their worst. 'Women grow irritable in the wind,' he said to himself as he passed the sideboard, and the stiff fruit, and made his way out of the dining-room to the stables.

At the time of the fire, my father had been a small boy, and he and his elder brother had been fetched down quickly from the nurseries so that their lives could be saved. Aunt Zita was up already, her small face was very white, it may have been that she felt already responsible for the fire. The old cook came into the long gallery to tell my father's mother of the disaster. The new electricity, which with the new running water in the house had meant a sudden, rash importation of warring elements, had burnt out its wires in the attics and lumber-rooms. The fine lamps, converted from porcelain Chinese urns, the polite chandeliers with glass fingers holding bulbs of electric light, were consumed by the primal fire, scorched black and then left to darkness. That night, my father's mother and her family stayed in the stables while the firemen leapt helplessly in the flames. The horses that had brought them on their wagons stood obediently in the stable courtyard. They were as black as funeral horses, and as the blaze died down and the house was gutted, they became invisible.

My mother and father came back into the dining-room, still in a state of confusion. Aunt Zita and I had only exchanged glances.

'You put that boy up to it,' my mother said to me. 'What's his name?'

My father was too angry to speak. His wing of chicken lay in front of him on his plate. The knife and fork lay across it, forming a barrier.

'You got Maurice to ring the bell,' my mother said.

Aunt Zita pursed her lips and then smiled. It was still dim

in the dining-room, for the leaves were coming down all the time in the winds, and falling in the Hen Pond and clogging the sluice, and I saw my mother strain to look at her, to see if she was encouraging me in this terrible prank. Aunt Zita's face told her nothing.

'Someone could have been killed,' my father said at last, 'running out to see what had happened. And there are tiles missing on the stable courtyard. In the dark, someone could have twisted their ankle.'

'But think, anyway,' said my mother, 'all the people from the village got up and came to beat out the fire. They thought it was a fire.'

'How?' I said. 'Where did you see them?'

'I think Maurice ought to go away somewhere,' my mother said as she looked at me.

'They were coming up the drive with sticks,' my father said. 'They must have gone the long way round, down the back road and through the field. They must have thought the stables could already be on fire.'

My father picked up his knife and fork and began to eat. He ground on the chicken as if punishing it for my and Maurice's misdeeds. With his usual practicality and unconscious cleverness my father had staved off two revolutions. This was how he saw his role in the house and on the surrounding land: as a pacifier and steward, only bringing down the fist when incompatible things had got together and had to be forced apart. By making the bell heard, he had transformed the villagers, who were resentful of the coming winter and the hard fields, into a helping band. And my mother and Aunt Zita, impressed by the sound of the bell, which had blotted out the wind, and which had come suffocatingly into the dining-room leaving a weight that for a time made them unable to speak, were quiet until the end of the meal.

So we finally ate in peace. But as the wind, cautious and sniffing at first, began to rise in the chimney, Aunt Zita turned to my father.

'I think it was the wind that got at the tongue of the bell,' she said.

At this my mother frowned. Aunt Zita drew a yellow envelope from her bag, which was on the floor by her chair.

'Whatever it was,' she said in her clipped, light voice, 'the bell has heralded a new arrival. You didn't know Wilhelmina was coming to stay?'

My father and mother rose together, as if some mechanism had sprung them from opposite ends of the table.

'Nor did I,' my mother said.

I followed Aunt Zita to the hall. There would be exclamations of horror at the telegram. I waited for the night journey over the sleeping village, and the school, and the magenta armies of Maurice's willow-herb beneath us as we flew.

Sometimes, when the big bell rang in that time of the year it meant the arrival of Aunt Thelma. Then my mother would look completely confused, as if the days had run backwards and the earth had tilted, spilling out the summer and sewing up the hole, the jagged rent being where Aunt Zita and Aunt Thelma would, unthinkably, find themselves in the house together. For Aunt Thelma came long after the first dark blue evenings and the north wind, after the Indian summer and the succeeding storms. She came in the politest part of winter, when a thin white frost covered the ground, and Aunt Zita had been long gone, and a few robins walked about on the grassy path, which by then looked like the shaven cheeks of a corpse. The bell that tolled her coming was low and melancholy. There seemed little hope of resurrection, either for the people who sat in their houses in the village in the long nights, or for my father and his family. The sharp, pointed lines of the hills, and the field flattened into lakes of frost, looked as if they would be incapable of softening and turning green again. Also, when Aunt Thelma came, the stars seemed to be brighter in the night sky, the white fields more ethereal below, as if a map of an unobtainable heaven had been spread out for her approval. My mother walked with her past the sweet-smelling filth of the cows, their tails hanging down over shit flanks and bulging udders, with an abstracted expression she had taken from her sister. The tall, weak-backed firs on the road to the lake half-stooped to her, like acolytes. But Aunt Thelma was fiercely contemptuous of worldly obeisance and pomp. Her clothing was as simple as sackcloth, and the smile she wore for the worldly relatives by marriage who surrounded my mother had all the false sweetness of the smile of martyrdom. It was very seldom that my poor mother found herself in the house with so explosive a mixture on her hands. Aunt Thelma, Christmas and Candlemas had come to be as familiar as the tattered calendar, each month crowned with a fierce loch, that hung in the schoolroom under the map of the world.

But if Aunt Thelma had equipped herself with another job, working in the staff kitchens of a war hospital maybe, frying three hundred and fifty eggs in one batch, cooking lean mutton in the bales of hay in the neglected grounds — then her dates would change and she would come at another time. Aunt Zita, for all the changes she brought with her, was immovable in her visit. Yet, as the end of the war came and evacuees were sent back to roofless towns and the wonderful new future opened, Aunt Thelma joined the Labour Party and her visits became more erratic. After dinner, as she ate her peach in the company of Aunt Zita, she seemed to eat into the peach like a maggot, destroying the glossy bloom and the sweet scent, which always reminded me of the balls we danced at, with Aunt Zita draped in a cobweb of gold silk. My mother watched them both, sighed, and lowered her eyes. Aunt Thelma's gold was different from Aunt Zita's – it was Christian gold, intangible as a halo. Aunt Thelma's dinner dress, which was like a surplice, was white, with a pale gold frill at the foot. Aunt Zita, scowling at her from her medallion gold, the gold that bought the slaves Aunt Thelma freed, the gold on which her profile was stamped, and the gold that made chains at her wrists and feet when she went dancing, saw her brother's sister-in-law turn her gold to base metal, and shut them all for ever in a world without precious ore, a world of paper equality. She would eat her peach faster than Aunt Thelma, and let the sweet juices flow unchecked down her chin.

My father took me out in the boat on the lake on these occasions of the coinciding visits; and he would sit looking up at the stony face of the ravine, as if searching for an answer. The pagan winds, unbothered by Aunt Thelma's coming, blew into the narrow lake like a funnel. The boat skittered on the water, which was made up of a million ripples as fine as hair. My father sat with the oars flat out on the water either side of him, in a gesture of resignation. Waves the size of minnows rippled under the oars. The winds dodged the boat round the small islands and then out into the main channel again. Aunt Zita's stormy autumn was in full progress. In the stern clouds, grey as fuselage, I saw shreds of night, brought on early by Aunt Zita's impatience to leave the house, get away from Aunt Thelma, and visit the ball. 'We will have much less than we had,' my father said. But he would say nothing further. He rowed strenuously against the wind, although it would have made little difference which direction we had taken, and steered the boat into its dark kennel at the side of the boathouse. From the rocking boat inside the building, which was like being on an uncertain bed in a dream, we looked out at the loch and the clouds closing in over the hills. Aunt Thelma had shrunk the lake already, and squeezed the valley in her iron fist.

At these times of strain, when half the house had a pious, austere air, and the William Morris printed curtains and carpets glowed with Aunt Thelma's sanctity, and the chairs grew tall-backed and uncomfortable and pressed in with admonishing arms, Aunt Zita's domain took on a tatty, theatrical look, like a child's cardboard theatre. The hall, with its christening scenes and the stained glass windows that came and went with the flashes of sun outside, the rainbows in those stormy days throwing sudden pietas, blood on the face of the dying Redeemer blazing for a moment before the obscured stables opposite, blue eyes of female saints that danced in the high windows – the hall took on a more delicate appearance, as if the Gothic were true Gothic and the stone masons and sculptors, as they wrought the thin arches and crusader knights, had been true believers. The clumsy imitation that my father's grandfather had put up, the travesties of purity and faith in the coy, Victorian gargoyles, the assertion of money and power, were transformed by Aunt Thelma. My father's family, if they were seen wandering in the house, looked repentant and bowed.

Aunt Thelma took pity on one of my father's aunts, who had died young after trying to run away with a penniless man, and she sat sometimes with her in a remote bedroom that looked out over the courtyard, the faded chrysanthemums of the late Victorian wallpaper nodding like cabbages when the flickering sun went in there. Aunt Zita's gold, tasselled cushions, and the tables of Venetian mirror she restored to the unused gallery, and the chandeliers which threw bubbles of white light on the walls, looked impossibly vulgar and unnecessary. In the evenings, under the dim lights, while Aunt Zita's fire raged and she tapped her foot on the floor to the sound of secret ballroom music, Aunt Thelma talked to my mother of their childhood in a low pleasant voice. My father was utterly excluded. He looked up at the dead game and piled fish in the dining-room pictures, each framed with the heavy gilt his grandfather had loved, and his eyes were as frozen in surprise at the sudden ending of life as those of the tumbled birds. Then when he could have had Aunt Zita without my mother caring, he ignored her completely. Perhaps he knew that with the coming of Aunt Thelma, and the stamp of a false winter that came down with her, he no longer had his elder brother as a rival. For Aunt Thelma made sure that Aunt Zita's visits to the nurseries were stopped. In the room where the pigeons waited on branches, and the clusters of berries were half-pecked away by damp and age, Aunt Thelma's religious ceramic had swollen out over the fireplace. Aunt Zita and my father's elder brother, if they tried to embrace, felt themselves turned to porcelain sinners, cracked as Aunt Thelma's Madonna billowed above them in her robes.

The only diversion, as Aunt Zita waited in agonising longing for the return of the north wind, was a bomber, gone astray from its target, which flew over the village and house and valley. It landed in boggy ground in the high hills above the lake, making a crater that was deep and round with the heather torn away at the rim. When Maurice went up there – to find the bomber, he thought, to rebuild his toy fighter planes with the metal and to look long at the dead body of the pilot, strapped into his cockpit, his dead fingers on the buttons that would have guided him back to Germany – he stood disappointed in the short grass and heather and scuffed with his toe on the fresh earth at the edge of the hole. There was no sign at all of the plane. Nobody, in the heart of the war, would take the time to come and dig it out, and the enemy, and his bomb, and his broken machine were buried for ever in the soft peat above the loch.

The bomber had gone over The Street, and then over the lonely house where Maurice lived with his mother on the side of the hill along from the Hen Pond, and then, after darkening the school where the teacher sat correcting homework, it roared over our garden and into the hills above the ravine. Aunt Thelma and my mother ran out on to the lawn. But, in a world that was alive to Aunt Zita when she was at the height of her powers, and where the sound of the big bell could hang like a black cloud in the sky, there was no after-sighting of the vanished plane. It was an invention that had been super-imposed on the real, living world, and had been sent out to destroy it. Aunt Thelma and my mother put their hands up to their brows and craned into the distance, as if cutting off their minds from their eyes would enable them to see the enemy. Uncle Ralph, hearing the commotion from his laboratory in the turret, stood at his window with a telescope. The threat, which had never been grasped, had gone. Uncle Ralph went down to the Racket Court, trudging through the thick mud that grew in the windless, rainy days which often bound Aunt Zita and Aunt Thelma together, to look at his monoplane and envisage himself in battle against the Germans. Later, when the hole had almost healed over and a bonfire had been lit on the hill above the Hen Pond to celebrate victory, Uncle Ralph patched the flimsy wings of the plane on to its body and flew up the valley to the lake, at no greater height than the tops of the stooping fir trees. He had to circle the lake twice before he could rise to the extent of the ravine, and, once there, he flew over the shadow of the crater a hundred times, like an old bird searching for dropped prey. When Uncle

Ralph came back from these expeditions, Maurice would appear breathless in school, for he had run, hardly slower than Uncle Ralph's plane, the whole length of the valley to the lake, to watch the reconnoitring.

Aunt Thelma brought a different life to the people of the village. After the victory bonfire, which was in the bright summer and therefore free from the intervention of Aunt Zita, the houses in the village began to change, and Aunt Thelma stayed often with my mother then. The occasional ghostly return of my father and Aunt Zita's family had a disastrous effect on the villagers, and ruined the new spirit which Aunt Thelma was hoping to instil in the farm. When my father's mother in her soft, long, simple dresses wandered along The Street, smiling and nodding her head to the neat old-fashioned gardens, the sweet william and lupins, glancing at the dark windows of uneven glass where she could see only herself reflected, but where the inmates saw her inquisitive eye as wide as the sky – there was a return to the old ways of keeping the houses, without indoor sanitation or the new lino, and wallpapers as smart and polite as polished veneer. Aunt Thelma went up to The Street to banish the old habits of the route my father's mother would take when she wanted to walk to the Hen Pond. Sometimes Aunt Thelma flouted my father's elder brother as he wandered bewildered at the reconstruction of the labourers' cottages. His friends stood with him in their straw hats with blue ribbons. They stood about in the farm and lounged on the hay bales. Slipping on the cow dung in the sloping field above The Street, they laughed at the utility fittings and bright nylons that were being taken into the renovated homes. Aunt Thelma shooed them away, and they went jesting and nudging down the mossy steps to the farm steading, where they disappeared at the muddy crossroads by the byre. If Aunt Zita was there it was hard to get rid of them – and in those times when there was talk of land belonging to everybody, and the valley no more under the long entails of my father's grandfather, my father was as much responsible for the restoration of his family as she was. My mother, torn between loyalty to her husband and belief in Aunt Thelma's measures, kept well away from The Street. In Peg's shop she stared absently at the new orange wallpaper and shiny brown paint, and made no reference to the bathroom, the first the cottage post office had seen, that had been wedged in next to the tiny sitting-room on the ground floor. Peg, however, soon lost her air of modernity. The cats settled on the chocolate-bar boxes, and the dust that came down again on the new lino went as before into the pale bars of the electric fire, giving off a smell of singeing hair.

In the time before the hills took in the bomb, and while Aunt Zita was waiting for the north wind to rise again, we went to the Hen Pond almost every day; and at some point we took Uncle Wilhelmina with us, for he had arrived unexpectedly and the yellow telegram, delivered by Peg in innocence to Aunt Zita rather than my mother, had given no more than a few hours' notice. Uncle Wilhelmina stood by the short, artificial shore of the Hen Pond with a pained expression on his face. The slab of water, apparently animated by mechanical ripples, was unappealing to him. The clouds going fast across the sky did not reflect in the waters of this reservoir from which the dynamo drew its power. Uncle Wilhelmina seemed to lean against the wind as if it were a stuffed bolster and could be depended on to support him. His nose flared out and one lurid cheek was presented in profile.

Although my father hoped not to have to go to the

expense, the blockages in the Hen Pond had reached a level where Uncle Ralph's anticipated draining had to take place. The water went out more quickly than Uncle Ralph had imagined, and he looked downcast almost at the lack of drama, and the empty pond like a gash in the side of the hill, with some small fish smacking against each other in the agony of air, and old bootlaces which Uncle Ralph at first claimed were eels. Some of the men from the farm poked the leaves away from the sluice with sticks. They lifted the wooden sluice gate and took it out altogether. Uncle Ralph rubbed his hands as the water went down into the thin burn with a roar and spat up at the banks which were high, with small precipices and cliffs. The dying fish nearest the sluice went down, belly up. Uncle Wilhelmina still stared at the sky, as if relief would come to him from the clouds, or from the hostile peewits, which shrieked and moaned over their invisibly demarcated land.

Aunt Zita, when all the family went to the Hen Pond, stood on her own on the narrow ridge of unnatural sand at the far end from the sluice and looked out at the water and her relatives as if she were on a short holiday at Lac d'Annecy. She would wear one of her hats with feathers on these occasions, and was counting on the feathers, perhaps, to act as a weathervane, for when they began to toss violently in a wind that was coming round increasingly to the north, she smiled to herself and then at her brothers. When the feathers were still, seeming against the steep side of the hill to be growing like black thistles out of the ground behind her, she frowned and stared down at her slender anklestrap shoe on the beach. Then, for want of anything better to do, she summoned her elder brother, and my father's mother, and she stood with them on a piece of driftwood which from a distance looked like a smart pier, a jetty from which they might all embark on a steamboat cruise on the lake. My father's elder brother would appear astonished if Uncle Wilhelmina was there, for he had last seen his youngest brother when he was dressed in long white gowns, with ribbons in his long, golden hair.

'Shall we go on the Tuesday walk?' my mother said. She added that there was time, if we left now, to go along the side of the hill and do the Tuesday walk 'properly', by returning in time for lunch along the back road. Uncle Wilhelmina at once burst into a shrill laugh.

'I shall go home,' he said. 'And then – I must say I have ordered the car – I shall leave!'

Uncle Wilhelmina walked back alone to the house from the Hen Pond, picking his way over the relics of a slate quarry and through sudden patches of reptilian green where water ran under the ground. His suede boots were purple and fringed with Robin Hood streamers; the height of the heel would have taken him down the long galleries of Versailles, over the bone-dry parquet, and, returned by the mirrors set in solar systems of gold leaf, he would have appeared as a receding army. But in the hills, where the distant ridges of the mountains followed each other monotonously, and were sometimes interrupted by ridges of cloud that looked as if they had come up like hot vapour from their flanks, Uncle Wilhelmina seemed alone and absurd. Lacking a reflection, cut off from the shadow courtiers who looked back at him from the depths of his glass, he stumbled over the burn by the grey stone wall that separated farm from hill. He wandered along The Street as he had done half a century ago with his mother, when with her eye she seized the windows and with her hand took bread and mittens from a rush basket. The people from the village looked at him without interest. Uncle Wilhelmina's suit was made of cloth of gold, but no one in the village was interested. Nor did Uncle Wilhelmina pay the slightest attention to the innovations in The Street, the indoor toilets that were beginning even in the war to be installed, and the bright wallpaper covered in triangles and birds and dots.

Uncle Wilhelmina came for his few visits in a big car driven by a chauffeur. The chauffeur went outside the valley, to find an inn where he could stay while he waited for Uncle Wilhelmina to decide when he wanted to go back. Uncle Wilhelmina took a long time to get into the house, and his cages of birds and boxes of lizards were carried up by the driver and by Minnie to his room. Immediately he released the birds, but it was some hours before they flew against the windows in a desperate attempt to get south. They were crushed by the journey, and sat on the fender in Uncle Wilhelmina's room, behind which Minnie had lit a coal fire. The lizards, which appeared on the backs of chairs in the hall and along the gilded frames of pictures long after he had gone, escaped early from the big room under Uncle Ralph's where Uncle Wilhelmina was always put, and their bright blue eyes jumped like blue fire from their hiding-places. Minnie wrung her hands when she saw them going up the wall, tree-lizards whose blatant green was quite incapable of adapting to the chrome walls and plaster cornices.

Uncle Ralph classified his dead objects fifteen feet over the head of Uncle Wilhelmina's live reptiles and aviary, and it may have been this unsuitable closeness that ended Uncle Wilhelmina's visits so suddenly – or the silver birch tree, the only one of its kind that grew so near the house, which tossed its thin branches and small silver-green leaves incessantly at his window, making a sound like the sighing feathers in Aunt Zita's hats. At any rate, he always went as unexpectedly as he came. Sometimes he forgot a bird – a macaw or a Java sparrow with a beak as thick as a wooden whistle, and they circled and cried on the upper landing, where there was a skylight and the illusion of escape. Then, the deep house below turned to jungle at the sound of their sudden, spitting cries, and the ghostly maids who danced attendance on Aunt Zita swayed in their attic rooms like birds caught in a net of creepers.

On the night that Uncle Wilhelmina arrived, the great bell was sounded by the wind in the granite *campanile* intended by my father's grandfather as a tribute to Renaissance glory – the achievements of those great philosophers and artists being equal in his mind to his own. The railways which lay like cracks across the placid face of his country, the factories and mills that shoved their snouts to the sky, and which bore his name, the portraits he had had painted of his thin-faced daughters and brown-haired wife whose parting down the middle of her head divided her as neatly as an apple – these were his joy and pride. And on that night, when the bell rang out and the wind began to climb in the chimney, Aunt Zita went off to her second ball, and I with her.

'I haven't got a room ready for Wilhelmina as I didn't know he was coming,' my mother said. 'He can go in the Lavender, I suppose.'

This went unanswered. My father peeled an orange, and the pith floated down from his fingers to his plate. Aunt Zita lit a cigarette. We rose without coffee and went into the hall to greet my father's youngest brother. Minnie was there, heaving a birdcage. She had never liked Uncle Wilhelmina. A tall black bird, with wings folded like an umbrella, looked out at her. Uncle Wilhelmina followed, in a suit with several pockets and a small silk handkerchief fluttering from each one. In this way, he resembled a conjuror's trick – and Aunt Zita smiled at him for a moment with a certain fondness before she remembered her own magical performances, and the strenuous night that lay ahead. I saw her wonder whether Uncle Wilhelmina's arrival would spoil her ball – and I saw her decide she would not let this happen. Aunt Zita's shoulders went back, and the soft blue flame which had been licking round her since the growing of the wind, went out in a display of gold, and the vivid green that can sometimes be seen in the depths of a fire, and feathers of pale red. Aunt Zita, gracefully bowing and placing her small feet with the precision of a peacock, moved away from Uncle Wilhelmina and across the hall. The gold fire round her bounced off the walls and ceiling like droplets of wine.

In the sitting-room, where my mother had hoped to sit quietly with her needlework, occasionally glancing at my father to see whether he had fallen asleep or not, and where Aunt Zita had hoped to gather her spirits for the long ride on the back of the wind, changes had already been brought about by the coming of Uncle Wilhelmina that distressed my mother and father very much, and made Aunt Zita give off a loud and uncharacteristic laugh. Uncle Wilhelmina, having said he was tired, had gone to his unaired, vaulted room with his birds and his long boxes of lizards – but he had spread already in the house the strongest secretions from his skin, the waves, as violently coloured as Aunt Zita's, from his wandering mind. In his spectrum, the house lost all finite qualities and, roomless, wall-less, sprawled in the contours of a tent over the forbidding valley. It was impossible to see to the end of the folds of desert-wide striped silk, Bedouin soft ceilings and sagging walls without corners. Uncle Wilhelmina's scarlet parrots flew high in the air. Bunches of artificial roses and violets lay on the wildly patterned strips of carpet in the sand. There was a smell of the circus, and a dryness from the wind outside that made Aunt Zita's nose twitch; and standing about bemused were men in blue and white aprons, and my father's mother and my father's elder brother. Then, as the image faded, and my mother made her way to the usual armchair (which she chose so as not to have to share a sofa with Aunt Zita), my father said:

'Wilhelmina looks quite well, I think.'

Aunt Zita rose. She seemed shaken but determined. I saw her glance quickly round the room, with its staid furniture and William Morris prints on the curtains and chairs, and I saw her realise that her mother – my father's mother – who had so loved her youngest son, who had poured her love into him after the death of her eldest, had gone after him, in search of him perhaps upstairs. And in Aunt Zita's jealousy, when, running with her brothers, she had fallen on the concealed iron ring of the door in the grass and made a long-forgotten scar on her leg – in the jealously of half-remembered rebuffs, and the cries behind the Racket Court when the youngest brother was scooped into his mother's arms, and the dark trees round the field where the ice house had been planted in the ground, Aunt Zita took me fiercely by the arm and led me out of the room with her. My mother looked up, tried to stop me with her eyes, and sighed.

The upper part of the house, as Aunt Zita had suspected, was a jungle now rather than a cocoon of desert silk to keep out the bright blue, metal nights. Creepers swung in ropes from the spiral staircase that led up to Uncle Ralph's room where he lay in hiding like a sloth, unable to bear the meeting with Uncle Wilhelmina. There were too many birds in the air, and they seemed also to spiral as they flew, wings beating, like a column of fiery smoke towards the dusty skylight in the roof. There was a smell of French tobacco. And the men in blue and white aprons stood in the recessed doorways of the rooms ... and as we ran, Aunt Zita and I, to the nurseries, we saw the trail of artificial violets on the bumpy carpet in the corridors, and a smear of blood on the speckled black lino of the nursery bathroom, where my father's eldest brother looked out from his club and his straw-hatted friends ... and we ran, to the room where once the faded yew berries had waited for Aunt Zita and my father's elder brother. Now there was red velvet on the walls, and mirrors that threw back the shifting limbs and shadows of waterfront brothels, and a chandelier that looked like dangling gold paper. Aunt Zita moaned with disappointment. Somewhere, beyond the scabrous mirrors, amongst the ruddy men, stout, and in their aprons striped like closing blinds, my father's eldest brother was drawn into the sink of Uncle Wilhelmina's life. His strictness gone, his sweet adherence to his principles removed at one blow, he lounged for ever in a smoky room above a quay, with pimps and harlots and criminals, with all the restless, heaving tripe of humanity that could never be imagined in this narrow alley, peopled as it was with whey-faced men and women hard in their work and morals. Aunt Zita gazed after him in anguish. I supposed my father's mother must be in there too, pale and out-of-place as an English water-colour in that bar. She would be searching too, but this time for both her sons, who had slipped into her maternal nightmares of homosexuality, hashish and release.

Aunt Zita took me to her room, so that we could dress quickly for the ball. We rose in the spiral staircase beside the birds, and we listened for the wind, which was subdued by their cries and the frantic beatings of their wings. But we could hear it there, like the grey breakers of a running sea on the walls of the house.

My father's mother had had a wooden bird carved at the top of the coiling banister of the stair; and on its head, its wooden pelican's head, sat a cluster of humming-birds escaped from Uncle Wilhelmina's cages. The pelican pecked at its breast, to tear flesh to feed its young: I had often seen my father's mother standing there, the consequences of her feeding all round her in the house – with Uncle Ralph a few paces behind her in his Martian space chamber behind locked doors, and Aunt Zita, fretting in her black lace gown for the next falling in love at the ball, and my father sleeping, deep in the accounts of the farm, while my mother dreamed of Aunt Thelma. Now, the pelican stood rooted to its wooden column without her and the humming-birds made round nests in the skylight above its stern, bald head and plucking beak.

Aunt Zita's room had three steps leading up to it, and it was low-ceilinged, so that the birds, which came with the rising wind, and which flew along the passages, leaving trails of phosphorescence on the dim walls, knocked themselves on the low roof above Aunt Zita's head, their fire-bearing tails fanning out into a weave of fiery plumes. Sometimes, when Aunt Zita was getting ready for the ball, and the north wind was charging to get in, and her companions, her grotesques, the agents of her long journeys into memory, stood close to her as she wound the scarf of the night wind around her neck, to go into her room was like going into a cave of fire, or on to a dark island where, in the Icelandic night, an army of smiths and forgers thudded at their anvils and sent up sparks of flame to the polar stars. When the window was opened, and Aunt Zita stepped out on to the sinuous back of the wind, all the flames flickered and danced, like church candles. Then, when she had gone, the birds flew away down the passages again, making a stripe of pale red in the shoulders of the sleeping house.

The room next to Aunt Zita's was never opened, the key had rusted over, and the bell it owned in the basement never rang. It was the room of the daughter Louisa who had tried to run away; and on certain evenings, towards the end of Aunt Zita's visit, when the chrysanthemums were pale with continual rain in the garden, and the grassy path was mud, and there was green light from the sluggish, rolling clouds when Martinmas, and Aunt Thelma, and the season of repentance and bereavement were coming, and Aunt Zita's fire was fading, and the firebirds sat in dull, brown rows on the telegraph poles – then I would see my father's grandfather letting himself into that room, to visit Aunt Zita's aunt. It was said that he had never forgiven her. But if my mother put this forward at a meal, and Aunt Thelma looked up at the ceiling in sorrow and excitement, my father would munch his apple as if he had never even heard of the scandal. My mother was soon silenced: it seemed lascivious to summon dead love, and Aunt Thelma, anxious to show her interest in the house and the enclosing valley, would say:

'When are we going up to have a picnic tea at the loch?'

Louisa had been walking in the hills and plateaus above the ravine when she saw a figure coming over the crest of the mountain. She was searching for wild flowers for her collection; on the lower slopes she had found harebells, and pale yellow poppies with fragile petals that looked as if they had had the blood sucked out of them. On the heights there was only white heather to be found, or cloudberries like women's lips.

The man who walked down the creek in the ravine came from the other side of the mountains, from the stony land around the Yarrow. If my father and mother and Uncle Ralph made an expedition there – for Uncle Ralph claimed it was a good place to find meteorites, fallen stars for his classification – they had to drive the long way round, for it was a hard walk over the mountains to get there. Also, along the crest of the mountain was a line of seven stones, which marked the murdering-place of seven brothers, struck down by seven brothers of the rival tribe for running off with their womenfolk. My father went up to the stones only when he absolutely needed them. In order to suppress the rumblings of the valley, to bring peace to the house torn by Aunt Zita and my mother, he would go up to the stones and stand beside them. Then the stone men, fearless stone princes, marched down on the overlapping circles of the house and valley. They were inescapable, and even the north wind lurked in the trees when they passed.

Louisa didn't know that the man coming down the side of the hill to meet her had come out of these stones. She talked to him for a while, and he found her a sprig of white heather, which showed as a greenish glow in the duns of the mountainside. He had very black hair, and looked like a Spaniard. Louisa fell in love with him, and he told her it would be best for both of them if they met in the ravine on the following day and ran away over the mountains, out of her father's power. He told her he could find work as a shepherd to the south of the Yarrow, where the hills and wandering burns had never heard the sound of my father's grandfather's name, or his railways carrying merchandise to the north.

My father's grandfather would have nothing of a daughter of his marrying a shepherd. He overheard poor Louisa's plan, as she confided it to a sister in the nursery, where the berries on the interlocking branches were still fresh and red, and time hadn't yet pinched and withered them. He sent his factor, and two men from the estate office with guns, to frighten off Louisa's suitor and bring her back. When she was captured she was locked in her room. The flowers on the wallpaper, with their round, curly heads, were frightening

75

and oppressive. On the third day of her confinement there, she went out of her mind. And on the third day her lover came to the ravine for the last time.

Louisa lived to a great age, insane. She ate mostly in her room, but when my father was a young man and was responsible for her, she came down on certain occasions. This was before my mother's day, and Aunt Zita's Aunt Louisa had died by the time my mother found herself there – but my mother would say to Aunt Thelma, as my father sat without listening, that she had seen a very old man in Yarrow, when she had last gone on an expedition there, and that she thought he was a descendant of the family of the stones, and had been Louisa's lover. She said he had high cheekbones, and a lot of white hair, but you could see he had been very dark. He had been whittling at an elaborate shepherd's crook, such as they use in those parts. But my father would look straight ahead of him, and it was left for Aunt Thelma to say, with a particular shudder:

'How extraordinary!'

The trail Louisa had taken, down the valley where trees uprooted by the new force of winter gales lay with their stumps up in the soft poultice of fresh red earth, and the sides of the hills seemed to lean away from each other as they grew nearer to the loch, to the gape end of the road, was our way, on the night of the second ball, when the cruel week of limbo summer had passed and the equinox had got into the muscles of the wind, making it shout and stamp with fury. But it wasn't completely set in. It dropped its arms sometimes, and lay waiting. Then it renewed the tantrum, kicking at Peg's chimney pot until it fell, and slamming my father's study door so that the papers with neat figures, maps with contours in brown and green of the land, went into chaos on the floor and piled on top of each other. This was why Aunt Zita flew very low, although the

76

wind had been prancing outside her window tall and terrible as the shadow of a wolf – she didn't trust it yet to carry her straight up over the mountains without a fall.

In those years when the invisible war was taking place, and the German bomber pilot filled his nostrils with our soil, soldiers would appear in the valley and shoot at a target they had put up there, on the side of the hill. As we went along, in our train behind Aunt Zita, we saw the pale circles of the target and the bullet holes like dead flies on the board. Aunt Zita's grotesques leaned towards it, staring at the representation of death they saw there, abstract in contrast to their own fleeing, startling figures. If the moon was high, it was possible to see the soldiers, their ghosts, in khaki, firing at the abstract enemy and then falling, shot themselves, into drifts of brown leaves blown off the trees by the north wind. On those nights, when the moon was round and white above the target, a gentle face appeared in the pale, concentric circles. The black holes from the bullets made clusters on its mouth and eyes.

When two winds met in the valley, and the cross-currents brought all the disruption in the village to a head, and summoned Aunt Thelma in Aunt Zita's visit, and it was dangerous to leave for the ball because the north wind, meeting an assailant, a shower of icy arrows from the east, might well drop down, then the stone men marched from their burial ground to restore order. From the sparse heights where Louisa had hunted for flowers and met her ill fortune, they came down with the majestic dignity of a landslide. Birch trees and elders swooned and fell in the passage of their great stone legs. They cast dolmen shadows ahead, on the half-cut larch woods, and on fields which were already taking their first sheet of frost. Aunt Zita would rise above them, with the wind as her broomstick, and we held tight to the fluttering, ribboning flanks as we went. In their course, they trampled the soldiers, who put up a volley of fire and then ran away. These cairn men, who had been victims of sexual murder, and who had bled to death on the mountain, slowly petrifying, transmogrifying to stone, were unconquerable. The village heard them coming, as animals hear the first shifting of an avalanche.

On the night of the second ball, when we had cleared the black water of the loch and had risen into the ravine, the stones were still there, firmly in the earth. The moon was above them, with a weeping face, blotted with shreds of cloud. Louisa was dancing in the stones, weaving in and out, a dance like Strip The Willow. Aunt Zita knew, from her demented dancing, that Louisa foretold calamities, and that the night would end badly. The shadow of the stones fell across Louisa like a hood. Her dance, now far beneath us, was an omen that wrote itself on the flat crest of the hill, her tiny black figure crossing and looping in the stones.

In the years when the war kept Aunt Thelma from coming too early, and autumn had driven us back to the school-house, we sat at our desks, castaways, and the dark fog folded over the rigging on the trees outside. The trunks moved and the mist slipped between them like sea spray. In the pitted bark, where branches had been lopped to give more light for the teacher, we saw the round, horrified eyes of wrecked monsters. The green bracken, which was always exhausted at this time of year, gave off a whitish breath and rose in a rancid sea to our windows. Yet the teacher taught us the Magellan Straits, and Madagascar, and the spice islands. She didn't see the sea outside. In the lassitude of this part of autumn, before the spume of the bracken turned to orange and the trees recovered their hard edge, the sea filled the whole of the valley with its green body. Sheep grazed on its flanks. The village lay buried beneath it as if it were the future, in its volume the accumulation of a thousand years. Men and women had a fish look, and their mouths were round as they gaped for air in the terrible humidity. At this time, which filled my mother with weariness and my father with philosophical sayings, the house would grow gradually empty and quiet. My mother and father went south. I was sent to Willie and Minnie's, where my dog lived at the time of Aunt Zita's visits. And when I left the school and stepped out into the air that smelt of soaking weeds, I went in the opposite direction from Maurice. He went up the hill, past the Racket Court and past our house, where the rooms, their walls looking down now on tables masked in white sheets, had lost their purpose altogether. I went down the hill, on the slime, to Willie and Minnie's and the row of kennels with barred iron gates, and the dogs that leapt and barked at the sound of Willie's steps.

The dogs led very different lives from Willie and Minnie. In Minnie's front sitting-room there were round poufs covered in rust velveteen, and a settee with a grin of white lace fixed over the back, and rugs on the lino by the fire. There was a smell of baking, and of Minnie's grey flannel skirt that scorched slightly when she bent by the flames, in her dance with ash and poker. Round satiny cushions popped up behind visitors' heads when they sat down, like sudden haloes. Even the table was accommodating, dropping and raising flaps for food or games of whist. The dogs would never be allowed in here. Whereas in the big house my dog could run uncontrollably from room to room, and stop at the scent of my father's mother, or the pale aura of an aunt hovering by his chair, before dashing to a corner and rolling on her back, here her presence would be a threat to Willie and Minnie. When the summer went, whipped by the north wind, the dogs still ran in cells open to the sky, and when it rained they went in through arches to small rooms and a chipped enamel bowl. They seldom sat. In Minnie's room, when Joe from the town came to call, he was seated immediately and with ceremony. The little skirts of protective material on the arms of the chair swirled as he came down on the seat between them. The barking of the dogs went on through the opening conversation, as if the sound might alert him to their plight. But he talked on. When his second cup of tea was gone, he would open the bag propped beneath him and show them what he had brought.

Joe was overseer at the mill in the town. It made sweaters and cardigans and 'golfers', from the wool of the sheep that were allowed to wander on the hills and were sometimes rounded up by my dog, to find themselves pressed in a round stone room, awaiting nothing. The mill used cashmere, too, and this Aunt Zita liked, for its long journey from India, and the soft touch which made my father say, if he bumped against her in the hall:

'What's that nice thing you're wearing?'

It was understood that Joe could go fishing on the lake if he kept my mother and Aunt Zita supplied. But he was a friend of Willie and Minnie's, and he kept the best treasures for them. The 'fault' that labelled a precious cashmere a reject would be small in the gift offered to Minnie, no more than a spider's leg that had strayed on an underarm seam. For Willie he brought thick V-necks, machine-spun from the home-grown wool. They were the colour of tea, the colour of the burn that came down from the sluice at the Hen Pond after too much rain, or a dead green like the fields and bracken in these suffocating days. Joe said the fish suited the weather. They jumped out of the water at the fly as if they hardly knew what they were doing.

On a day that Joe called, I was allowed to free my dog from the kennel and take her up to the lake with him. The black dogs used by Willie for retrieving fallen birds growled at this release. They ran through the arches in the hope of the sound of the bucket at the back, and Willie with his hands stuck in oatmeal porridge. But there was no sign of Willie there. It was dark and cold at the back of the Kennels, and the lid of the barrel was on. The black dogs ran back into their cement cells. It was growing dark outside the Kennels, and the sky bulged with the rain it was still holding back, and shoals of midges went past their heads. The dogs set up a terrible howling.

Willie, Minnie and Joe paid no attention at all. They were sitting, and a heap of ladies' cashmeres was at their feet. There was a coral colour, and a Madonna blue, and a bright sea-green. Willie was smoking his pipe and tapping the bowl. The clock ticked loudly when he did this, and it put the three of them into a greater silence. Joe picked up each garment with care and handed it to Minnie for the choice. Although the town was small, and set down like a grid-iron in the one flat stretch between the hills, it was quite clear that Joe came from there and not from our valley. He always had a faint fever of the town on him, a hectic glaze. In the rowing-boat on the lake, his blue suit shone brightly. There was something venal in his plump fingers, in his cloth-soft tobacco pouch, and in his after-shave that smelt of the raspberry spirit Aunt Zita drank before setting off in her night-fire. I knew he went to the Saturday dances in the hotel just outside the town. The constant proximity of others made him quick and deft. Even when he sat in the boat on the lake, and the wind tugged his white hair and stood it up in soldiers before letting it fall again, Joe's eyes were always shifting. But to be with Willie was to see the blank gaze of a hawk.

It was almost dark by the time Joe and I were up the mud road to the lake, and that was because my dog had broken into the sitting-room and caused consternation. She had grown tired of waiting on the slope of grass that separated Willie's back door from the Kennels. The black dogs bayed at her, so she jumped in through the scullery window, and then they were silent, as if the incredible audacity of what they had seen had taken away their barking for ever. She ran from the scullery with her muddy paws. Minnie shrank back, and Joe went quickly for the cashmeres, and no harm was done, but my dog had to be put outside again before we could leave the house, to ward off bad luck. So Willie fed the black dogs, and after a while Joe and I went and stood with him as he stirred the oats, and Minnie swept where my my dog had been, a kneeling prayer to the god who watched over her home. As I followed Joe up the short drive from the Kennels and on to the road, I saw her in the upstairs bedroom she had shared with Willie for thirty years. The light was on behind her, and she held a feather duster as if she were con-ducting an orchestra of inaudible music. Then she turned, and waved the tips of the feathers on to the photos on the chest-of-drawers. They tickled the dustless photos of herself and Willie. At the secret signal that her silent music had stopped, and she was working ordinarily again, the black dogs burst into a barking that reached halfway up the valley, and came back in an angry shouting from the hills.

When my dog ran into Willie and Minnie's house, she ran in as if she was at home there. She didn't rush in circles, as she did in the big house, nor did she stop suddenly at the flicker of the dead, the edge of light which only she could see. She came into the unending present where Willie and Minnie lived; and it seemed without barriers until Minnie threw her out. Willie and Minnie were allowed no ghosts. The house wasn't even theirs. The keepers who had lived there before them might have been their ancestors, but it was of no importance. They had only their own youth to haunt them. In the photos, which were every day protected from the silt of the unchanging days, Willie was upright and his eyes were soft, as if he were looking at something that had just been offered him. Minnie's chin was pointed, and her face smiled from eyes to mouth. Now Willie's brows wriggled in his head and his cheeks had half fallen, the buried half coming up white under the jowls. His eyes could see only vermin and wide skies. And a web of wrinkles had caught Minnie's smiles. The real existence of the couple was more frail than the life in the corridors and rooms of the big house, where my father's Aunt Louisa, and his elder brother, and his mother who sat sewing when Aunt Zita came, had their names in porcelain by the bells that rang at their command in the basement. Their descent was in red and gold books in the library. In the directory, attached by a string to the telephone table under the bells, there was no name given for Willie and Minnie. There was a list of Keepers' Cottages, and the Kennels came fourth. A number; but anyone could have answered it.

When Joe and I, and my dog, had got up the valley, and opened the boathouse, and pushed the boat out on the water, Joe sat down heavily in the stern and opened his fishing satchel. He took out a fly and held it between the cushions of fat on his fingers. 'Yes, Willie tells me he's to get in moleskins for a coat,' he said. And, 'So you'll be making your turnips for the party soon. Getting quite excited, are you?'

The boat drifted out to the main channel of the loch and paused, while the conflicting eddyings under the prow slapped against the wood and rocked us into stillness. The absolute emptiness of the valley since my father and my mother and Aunt Zita, and all her band of grotesque night companions, had left, crept over the water and reached the tops of the hills. The larches rattled noisily: the wind had got to them but it wasn't with us yet. My dog ran on the sides of the ravines, and small stones dropped like sand in an hourglass.

I had seen the bodies of moles strung out on fences on the way up the valley. Their small, skinned corpses appeared once the big house was out of sight. They hung nose down, as if trying to get their snouts in the earth again, and throw up fresh tumuli. I knew the velvety grey fur would be stitched into squares for a coat for Aunt Zita. She would walk in the woods in it when the leaves were falling, and my mother would be deceived again, taking her for the grey of a silver birch tree, or an aspen. The moles would rot there, until they were no more than strips of tortured black leather. Willie might unstring them, if the smell attracted too much vermin for his traps.

In the village, as we went, the emptiness of the big house was spreading upward from the dale which embraced it, to the byres, and the square village building where the Hallowe'en party was held, and further, up the steps to The Street. Joe walked through the emptiness in his blue suit. A light was on at Peg's window, but she wasn't there. A pile of sweet cartons stood up against the curtain. From the house next door the cowman Jimmy came out and headed up the road to the byre where he worked. Peg had never liked him, because he was a leering man. He had lost his wife, and he lived with his daughter, who was thin and white-faced. Yet Peg was bound to him in a Siamese relation of stone and brick. She could hear his step at night, and know his cup of tea when he swilled it down and gasped. He seized the women in the village by the waist. Only the counter in the little post office stopped him handling Peg, and that was when he came in the front, to buy stamps or cola or a pad of Basildon Bond. Peg was afraid of her back step, adjacent to his and without the dividing line of officialdom. There, Jimmy would demand a packet of Weights after hours, and there was no sound of money in his pocket. She would turn him away, and he walked to the end of his path, to look bad-temperedly over the stone bridge to the ferns and nettles of the abandoned kitchen garden. When the big house was empty, and the emptiness had begun to rise as far as The Street and the cottage near the Hen Pond where Maurice lived with his mother, he was a terror in the village.

The absence of the strolling owners of the big house made the dogs and the children run wild in the village. Maurice was up half the night in the granary by the village hall, chasing rats with a shovel and bringing it down on their heads when they ran into corners. The other children raced with him. Even Peg's cats walked up the road to the hall and back, with their ginger tails sticking up behind. There was a clustering, from time to time, by the stained wooden notice board outside the hall. But it announced only a meeting of some kind, which had taken place in the summer.

The board presented a piece of history as the future. And in a time when people wanted news. For, in the unchanging-ness of the days, the absence from below in the big house made the evenings longer than usual, and the Hallowe'en party a flame that might seize the whole valley. If Aunt Zita was there, and the jostling of the north wind, they built the bonfire outside the hall with a special haste. They went right up the valley for wood. They made a toppling swan's nest, which on the night would let out an egg of fire. For all the authenticity of the victim, with Minnie's knitted hat on, and a thick body of crackling hay, and legs pressed in Peg's old lisle stockings, it was Aunt Zita they were going to burn.

It was possible to see, in the unlit twigs, the outline of her shrivelled neck and arms.

From the hall, I led the way into the valley short-cut which lay through the garden of the big house. Joe followed like a trespasser. If he had seen Willie there, coming up the path with the black dogs at heel, they would hardly have exchanged a greeting. In the near vicinity of the big house, the absence was oppressive. The green air, still untroubled by wind, hung around the long windows. From inside the house, set off perhaps by tripping, scattering feet, came a sound like wires being plucked, of the resonance of rooms in the emptiness. The house stood unnoticed on its carpet of turf, yet it gave out, from time to time, a groan from the chords inside.

On the loch, Joe caught a small trout. The dark, which had held off, made the fish invisible. He moved to the rower's seat; and the ends of the oars, which could no longer be seen, made an awkward pat on the water. The wind moved out of the larches at last. Joe wobbled as the boat rocked, and he strained for the open boathouse door. Up in the hills the German airman, the buried enemy, and the long rows of stone men took possession of the land. They brought thunder down with the wind, and the wild-cherry tree at the edge of the water shone out in a flash of blue. The airman was enormous, his shoulders took on the weight of the rain-heavy sky. Clods of earth fell from his nostrils into the ravines. And the mountains rang with the din of the stone men as they marched.

Under the floor of water in the boathouse, the weeds were as black as the drowned feathers in Aunt Zita's hats. Joe and I walked back along the valley, past the naked moles, and the great house stifled in its silence like a piano under a cloth. In the village, the bonfire had been half built, and forked twigs that had the brittleness of Peg's elbow stuck out at the side of it. Joe stopped at Peg's back door, to buy cigarettes. She came very slowly to the door, and the sweet orange smell, of spilt Kia-Ora, and the cats sleeping with their marmalade backs down, white stomachs uppermost in the shoe box, came out into the night. At this time, when my father and mother were away and everything was in abeyance, the wild nights that started in the mountains above the loch never came down as far as the village. They stormed, and then fell quiet again, and the wind did little more than ripple the surface of the bowl. So Peg had beads of water on her face, from the humidity, and the rushing sound, at her back door, of the burn under the bridge to the old garden, was as near as if it had been flowing through the middle of her shop.

Down the road, Minnie waited with tea and scones. The dogs, guessing my dog's arrival, sent a shivering howl. It went up past us, on a straight trail that held Willie and Minnie's souls too, to a change in the days, the jolt of the year's wheel turning. On the day the dead rose, the villagers' dead, they would go to the big house and fly into my father's mother's room. If the big house was empty, they haunted the Racket Court and decked themselves out in Aunt Zita's rotted velvets, in the cretonnes that had gone on the coughing aunts to the Pyramids, in the seal-fur coat Uncle Ralph wore in his monoplane and threw away when it grinned at the seams. They became bats, and when the exquisite remnants they had plundered from the Racket Court began to turn to dust, they settled in piles of leaves on the top landing of the big house. This was why my mother liked to be away at this time, if she could rid herself of Aunt Zita and if Aunt Thelma had not yet come. When the valley was in water, and after that, when the winds pulled at the nameless dead and set them dancing in the eyes of the turnips, she was afraid and weak. Even when there were people in the big house, the rising, forgotten dead could be seen jumping in the trees.

As we went down the last slope to the Kennels, the cowman Jimmy came up towards us. He was drunk, and flailing his arms. He must have walked five miles to the little town, to drink. Joe nodded to him. He stumbled on, and we arrived at Minnie's door. She was standing there in the coral cashmere she had picked. I hoped Jimmy wouldn't wander, in his drunkenness, into the grounds of the big house. He might circle there, among the changing gardens, and the ghosts of his own forebears gathered on the stone griffins and battlements. Or he might frighten himself, bumping into Uncle Ralph. Then, in his crazed state, Jimmy would do anything. The village, and Peg, would hardly be safe from him on the night of the labourers' dead.

Uncle Ralph, left alone in the big house, would often experiment with his own life at these times. When there wasn't a breath of wind outside, he would jump from his high window in a new flying-machine, and the thin wooden wings would carry him as far as the side of the hill opposite. He would lie panting for a while, in the silken cocoon he had constructed for his body. After, he would sit in a barrel of hot wax for nine nights and days, taking only figs to eat, so that when my mother and father returned his body was as soft and white as a caterpillar's, and he was ready, in his strange reversed vision of the world, to go into his winter chrysalis. Often, the experiments brought only the satisfaction of a mild danger to life. In the early morning, before the red postman's van came up the drive, Uncle Ralph stationed himself at the bottom of the cattle-grid, where last year's leaves, and sometimes a hedgehog, were imprisoned under two barred tracks. Uncle Ralph had the need to know what it was like to have a car going over him.

He crouched in the compost and waited for his sky to become thick with wires. When the underbelly of the van had passed, and clouds of exhaust still lingered overhead, he climbed out and walked stiffly back to the house. The van, on its return trip from depositing letters for my father, had to swerve to avoid Uncle Ralph, in his suit of autumn leaves.

When the last day of October came, and if my mother and father were away, I would still be at Willie and Minnie's for the night when the stone men hurled the winds down from the ravines, without any need for my father to summon them, and the bonfire raised the spirits of the working dead. On that night, the road from the Kennels up to the hall was so dark and wet that the schoolhouse was invisible, and the Racket Court beyond was the only faint shimmer. The fire that was unlike Aunt Zita's, the common, raging fire up by the hall, where the path from the gardens of the big house ran in a silken loop into the muddy road from the byre, lit the poaching dead as they helped themselves to the finery of the past. Then there was blackness. Egg-shaped stones came up out of sockets in the road and hit the soles of the feet. Minnie picked her way, in galoshes over court shoes.

The roads and paths of the valley moved together and apart again, on the night of this festival of return and re-animation. Our path, which was characterless now, neither fringed with the long grass that made a moving train of it, through the pampas land at the back of the house, nor white and cropped with winter, grew wider and sweet-smelling, and mist came down over it in a fringe. It came to fetch whoever would take it, by joining the back road before the hall came in sight. Closed in a vaporous tunnel, it snaked up past The Street and out on to open hill by the Hen Pond. There, it wavered suddenly. The grass was scratched and bare, the arms of the fog folded back to show the cottage where Maurice lived with his mother, and it lost direction under foreign stars. But it soon picked up again. The stone men were beginning to tramp the hills, and the sky was getting hard and bright. The water which had lain heavy poured out of the valley, like water going out from the Hen Pond sluice. It left heather springing in the new sharpness, and washerwoman's wrinkles in the valley bottoms where bulges of water still lay in the grass. The new path went thinly up through burnt heather roots to the source of the power of the valley. It climbed almost as far as the seven cairns.

Willie and Joe and Minnie stayed on the road up to the hall. I went to find Maurice. His mother lived alone in the cottage near the Hen Pond. A soldier found her in the town when she was a young girl working at the mill, and ever since she had been alone with a child at the Hen Pond cottage, and I never thought to look deeper than that. She had a pinched, sour face, and had to be forcibly taken down to the bonfire party, for she would rather have missed the fun. But there was respect for her in The Street. Her burden was understood. And she walked down The Street with heavy bundles, more often than not the washing she did for the oldest woman there, or a batch of baking for a friend, as if to emphasise her pinioned situation. She was the only woman in the village without a husband. Maurice's wild ways drew her mouth in even further at the corners, and on the night of the rising dead she looked as if she wished she could fly away with them, in a trail of rebellious fire against the sky.

When Maurice and I left his house, with his mother walking reluctantly behind and carrying a great black leather holdall, we followed the path to the gap in the wall and went down by way of The Street. Maurice's mother wanted to visit the woman of ninety, who was older than my father's mother would have been, and to call in on some of the other houses, to satisfy herself she was going to the party on the right day, and at the right time. The old woman, who had seen so much, sometimes told Maurice's mother of the worst Hallowe'en night, when there had been a scandal from the big house. If Maurice had been forced to go with his mother, he would listen to the scandal, and then there would be some version of it down by the chicken-house. But I preferred our own games to the ghosts in the brain of the old woman of ninety. We shivered with impatience in The Street, as his mother made her calls. There was light coming up from the square windows of the hall and the starting and stopping of an accordion. It even seemed the bonfire was about to be lit. We had to wait until Maurice's mother was ready, for if we left her alone she would go back to the Hen Pond cottage, and we would be punished for it.

The scene of the scandal was quite often enacted in the big house at that time of the year, if my mother and father were there and Aunt Zita still lingered, sulking in the water-logged days. It came to firm colour in the sitting-room, though shadows went sometimes to the front hall and even as far as the doorstep. It seemed that its shocking quality propelled it to leave the house and seek exposure: the shadows were grey and grainy, like lumps of newsprint. Even indoors, the colours of the scandal told by the old woman of ninety to Maurice's mother were sensational and vulgar. A comic book air filled the sitting-room, and the sofas and chairs, respectfully clothed in the tentacular flowers of Utopian socialism, were subjected to a crude overlay. There were aspects to the scandal, though, which the old woman couldn't have known. It contained an element of retribution. When the picture faded, it always went with the crashing of the stone men in the hills. A lurid, thunderous light crept into the house and we knew the green days were over. As the wind began to strip the trees outside, and the family scandal merged once more with the pure noses of pre-Raphaelite beauties, Aunt Zita would laugh at the annual rendering of her mother and brother's shame.

The old woman in the village had had a brother too, about the same age as Uncle Wilhelmina, and her brother was a half-wit. His thick lips were pulled back to the gum, and were ridged like the underside of a slug. Twisted words foamed from them. His eyes had been cut all wrong, so the pupils were rarely visible, and only the lichee whites looked out at the world. The old woman of ninety had cared for him, but he had died fairly young, age and time having formed a secret palimpsest in his body. By the time he was in his twenties, his head was reptilian, and his legs and feet still had the bumbling helplessness of a baby. In The Street and down by the byres he was seen only subliminally. He could have been the swish of a cow's tail, or the knowledge that a flock of pigeons has landed on the granary roof. He was never laughed at, at least by the people he lived among.

When my father's mother imitated the half-wit, there was a ripple of excited laughter from the sisters and sisters-in-law and some of the lady guests who had come in their chiffons to dinner from houses outside the valley. The men guffawed, as if there were something sexual and forbidden in aping the half-wit. And as she went on, my father's mother, freed for once on this eve of the rising of the village dead, shed her careful spirituality. She became pure vaude-ville. The bright, glaring colours that always returned when the scene was enacted, might have been arc-lights on her unspeakable act: Parma violet, red, and a yellow so strong it hurt the eyes. My mother always turned aside in disgust, she hated this garish play. But all the others laughed, in their titillation, as my father's mother blubbered at the lips, and dragged her elegant feet in such a way that they looked heavy and clumsy. And she broke into song, in a dialect that was just comprehensible.

Uncle Wilhelmina had left the room at the beginning of the show. No one had noticed, and even when the scene came back again and again in its scudding colours, it was impossible to detect the moment he slipped away. He went first to his room and made his face as white as a porcelain doll. He drew black spokes round the hubs of his eyes. He purpled his lips from a pot stolen from his mother's table. He looked as if he had drowned in cold water.

By the time laughter was rising in the sitting-room, and the butler was shooed away as he tried to announce dinner to a family and guests exalted by the public placing of their fears and confusions on the village idiot, Uncle Wilhelmina was out of the house and in the dark garden that was just beginning to be stirred by the wind. His white face, and long fair hair tied in a black ribbon, were all that was visible of him as he went up the garden. He paused by a weeping ash, and picked a switch. In the yew trees the village dead were collecting, and their faces looked out from amongst the fleshy yew-berries. Uncle Wilhelmina walked to the top of the garden, and let himself out of the gate by the hall. Mottled ivy pulled at his throat.

In the dining-room, the party had at last assembled. Rich food was handed round. When the constables from the town came in — it was then that the wind moaned more sharply in the chimney, and the picture began to fade, and the crackle of the coming winter put out the lethargy of the uncertain days. My father's mother's face went into an exquisite blur as the scandal was exposed.

Uncle Wilhelmina had wandered along The Street, soliciting. He held the ash stick in his hand and asked to be beaten. One of the cowmen, a man of indignation who was only a short time in the valley, ran all the way to the town to report the scene. And Uncle Wilhelmina was smuggled down to the house and up to his room, for charges were not in the end brought. He lay exhausted on his bed, with his blue eyes rolling in the white paste surround. The old woman of ninety certainly remembered seeing him out there, but she couldn't know of the travesty of her idiot brother in the big house, which came before Uncle Wilhelmina's arrest, and the unforgiving century of his mother's shame.

In the village hall, at the times when my father and mother and Aunt Zita were away, the people stood in clusters uneasily at first, for they were used to greater distances. Toffee apples hung from the rafters. The children butted them, raising bruises on the wrinkled heads. By the fire stood the accordion men, already scarlet in the face from the heat. When my family was there, our table was placed up near them, next to the fire, at the head of the hall looking down. A white cloth hung from its sides: the people from the village stretched out in a straight line from it, and at those times Jimmy didn't go up to Willie and say:

'Can I have the key, then?'

Willie handed over the key to the garage by the big house as if it had been my father who had asked for it. He knew, in the times of their absence, that Jimmy would reverse out the car over the fallen leaves on the checkered courtyard, that the leaves would rise again in the last swirl of wind before the end of the night and blow into the rooms and corridors of the big house, and that with the car at large we could all be in danger. Yet he handed over the key, in this ritual of Hallowe'en.

The car in the courtyard garage was a red car, built in 1914, and no one, not even Uncle Ralph, was allowed to drive it. My father's father had bought it in Austria as a collector's piece. It was the car in which the Grand Duke had been shot, in Sarajevo; and it was said to have killed over twenty people since. Each subsequent owner had crashed and died in it after only a few months. It had even pretended to break down once: its owner had arranged to be towed to the nearest town, and as they set off the engine sprang to power. It rushed into the towing vehicle in front, and crushed the impotent driver to death on the steering wheel. My father's father had been proud of this acquisition. It was shipped to England, as there wasn't a soul in Europe who would drive it by then for love or money. Uncle Ralph often stood for hours in the gloom of the garage and gazed at it longingly. He would willingly have sacrificed his life for the experience. But he was forbidden. After these feasts of contemplation, he went up to the gunroom over the garage and wandered about in the remains of my father's father's uninteresting museum. The adders pickled in bottles, and the black bear with an unconvincing red tongue, did nothing to distract Uncle Ralph from thoughts of the death car below.

Jimmy was the only man in the village wild enough to handle the car. With the big house empty, and Peg more and more apprehensive behind her weak barricades of cardboard boxes, he roamed the village at night. The inhabitants of The Street bolted their doors. Jimmy's manic phase was right ahead, with the first blast of winter wind from the hills, and he needed the red car. As the accordion band struck up, and we began to dance, we could hear it roar up the hill, turn with a demoniacal shriek at the cross-roads by the byre, and go off up the valley in a stream of pure, murderous noise.

Then the battle really started. The stone men, arming

themselves to conquer the valley while the house was undefended, found themselves charged, on the wide moorland, by the instrument of the greatest destruction of the century. Jimmy swerved between the cairns as if they were lamp-posts. The car, which had started the First World War, and so had sent my father's elder brother to his death, imprisoning my father in the valley and my mother with Aunt Zita, set out to destroy these early barons of the hills. Then it would have erased everything in its path. It carried the blood of thousands of years of plundered civilisations in its shining red paintwork. And Jimmy loved to be at the wheel of the car at the moment of its greatest confrontation, with men who had already been murdered, who were pure stone, and who knew nothing of the fine art and delicate spirit of the centuries it had already massacred.

In the hall, we danced and raised the spirits waiting to come in. Willie and Minnie danced together, with distant, concentrated expressions on their faces. I danced with Joe. He pressed me to the soft pillow of his stomach in a cashmere V-neck under the blue suit. We burrled, and the hall grew hotter, and the swinging toffee apples came down in puddles of melted sugar on the floor. Even Maurice's mother danced, and it was always with a woman from The Street, for this was the one night she could put her hand on the women, other men's wives, with whom she baked and knitted and talked, in an incessant stream, to the white smoke that rose from the kettle. Peg didn't dance, but she stood by the table where the refreshments were laid out, and she watched over the bottles of cola that had come from her shop, and the plates of bridge rolls. The souls of the nameless, field-labouring dead flickered in the candle eyes of the turnips on the wall.

Everyone heard the car when it roared back over the hills, and sighs of relief were muffled by the accordion thump.

Jimmy wasn't dead, nor yet had he crashed into the hall and finished off the celebrations. After he passed, someone dared to open the door and go out to set about lighting the bonfire. There was a new frost to the air already, and the black, poisonous smell of the death car's fumes.

If Aunt Zita and my mother and father were in the village hall, Jimmy couldn't get at the car of course, and his rage exploded elsewhere. As he couldn't exorcise the threatening spirit of the village at the time of decay and rot, the year turned sour for the whole valley after that. And if they were there, at the high table, and Aunt Zita's haughty fire cast a glow, the villagers sat patiently, waiting for them to leave. And the tension grew, that Jimmy would run out to light the fire before they were gone. For Aunt Zita, lolling against the chimney breast, looked more and more like a doll, ready to be thrown on the lighted sticks. We always went hastily, with Aunt Zita in her defiant whiteness amongst the flushed faces. Down at the house, we ate dinner under dim lights and to the thump, as if our hearts were dropping as we ate, of the accordion up at the hall.

It was only after years of going on the back of the wind with Aunt Zita that I came to understand how we never left the valley at all. The map of the world in the school, and the folds of the pale red continents washed by oceans, and the lakes like half-shut eyes in the green land-masses, were shut in our world, locked in our valley, which, with its circling hills, embraced them all. All the smells and spices of Aunt Zita's most exotic journeys came from Peg's shop: the ground nutmeg in a sample bottle that no one wanted to buy, and the palms, vivid over blue, on the wrapper of a coconut bar. All of time, which had pulled the land from under the sea, and nibbled at the cliffs, and seeded forests in the world on our map, was in the ancient mountains of our valley. All of recorded time, which had set men to pile stones, and hammer iron, and draw the exquisite wings of blue birds on pyramid walls, lay in the lines of the valley. In the Roman camp, where Uncle Ralph went to dig for coins, or segments of gold drinking vessels, centurions had sat in their interminable tedium, gazing out at the hills. Below the camp, where the hills went more gently towards the loch, the bones of animals preserved a million years made leaf patterns in the rock. In the village under the school, men long freed from the Romans armed themselves against the coming of the Hammer of the Scots. Steam from the first train went up into the clouds above our valley. And my father, locked in the soaring buttresses of his grandfather's dream, paced the confines of his land, from the stone effigies of the men who had fought to take it from each other, to the Romans yawning at their unprofitable empire, and back again to the castle of material gain. The world and history lay obediently within its bounds.

So, on the night of the bad omens, the night for which Aunt Zita had waited with such impatience, we flew the breadth of the world, and the world we had known at our first awakening opened up to us. In its fears, the night of storms took us to the hour of our birth. In the calm, ordered mansion where Aunt Zita danced in the tropical air, we knew the caress of infancy, the stately unchangeable march of the days.

It made no difference to Aunt Zita whether the night of her destruction was the night of the rising of the village dead, or a ball, so exactly like all the balls we had gone to, that the seed of her death could be seen only suddenly in the mirrors, or in a shifting arrangement of trees in the grove. But the time was marked, and she and her companions knew it.

When the night came, the fissure of evil opened. Aunt Zita danced ... with the young men, long dead in the wars, who stood close to her with thin, smiling lips ... she went to the grove, and the fire rolled from her on to the grass already wet with morning. As Aunt Zita laughed, and her eyes shone black in a southern night that could never throw off the frivolous light blue of its sky ... and her flames were caught and paraded in the mirrored ballrooms in silver torches ... as she leapt, the village made ready to burn her ... and the snow, hiding behind Pacific stars, prepared its blinding, annihilating descent. Aunt Thelma was coming. Louisa, emblem of carnal love denied, wove her mad patterns among the stones. Persecution and injustice rose with pitchforks, and marched on Aunt Zita as she danced.

Aunt Zita was quickly burned. She was subsumed in her own element. The people from the village dragged her by the hair, past Peg's shop, and put her on a pyre by the farm steading, where one road went off to the Tuesday walk, and the fabric of hill that hid Aunt Zita's family, and the other road went to the loch. She burned as quickly as paper. And in the small crowd was Maurice, and the forest of willow-herb hissing around him, and Peg from her dusty shop, her hair bound up behind her small head.

Aunt Zita's face hung for a while in the air, after the flames had eaten her. She looked suddenly like one of her imaginary companions – like a white paper mask, a moon-shaped kite with the night coming in the slits, for eyes.

The snow began to fall. It fell first on the heights, and turned the stones to shrouds. It fell on the Roman walls, and the bleak precinct of the camp. It fell on the fire where Aunt Zita was burning, and on the forests of larch and fir, and it gave its deathly kiss to the flowers in the autumnal gardens. It fell on the turrets of the house, and made pointed

white clown hats on the chimneys. It fell in at my mother's window, as she was brushing her hair before the start of the morning, and she turned and said to her face in the mirror:
  'Isn't it dark today?'

Aunt Thelma had come. The people in the house walked with reverent, bowed steps. The Gothic windows were filled with pale red light. In the hall, when Aunt Thelma summoned the christening scene, there was the smell of sanctity, and my father's mother fell to her knees and prayed. Beside the loch, in the damp afternoons while Uncle Ralph hunted in the shallow water for forgotten treasure, and the minnows played about his wrists, and my mother balanced an iron kettle on the smoking twigs, Aunt Thelma stalked Aunt Zita and my father's elder brother in the ragged wood and tore them apart with curses. The swans beat their wings on the black water when Aunt Thelma came. My father sat alone in his boat, staring up at the clouds in the sky.

When Uncle Wilhelmina made his sudden departure, his birds had flown to the place under the hill where Aunt Zita burned, to circle until the fire fell from their tails and they were no more than black crows, diving and flying in the winter sky. Then the house settled to its quiet, religious seclusion. My father, with the rich, painted food garishly behind his head in the dining-room, blinked at my mother and Aunt Thelma as they talked. In the valley, the white robe fell over the hills. It hid the Elizabethan gardens, and the animated forests, and the arena of memory and magic. It hid Uncle Ralph's fallen stars, and the traces of Uncle Wilhelmina's excess, and it sealed the house, to a crypt, to a marble tomb.

In the village, the men came home from fields so hard they rang to the sound of plodding feet. The women picked turnips that lay stinking, half a hairy monkey's head above the ground. They boiled them in water. On Peg's cards, which came tucked in envelopes that looked as if they had never been fresh, the snow was frosted with silver glue and the holly berries were attached to silver bells. Aunt Thelma walked on the frozen path, where in the summer the grass had been so long that it would have hidden her. The long, white summer was nothing to do with her. Her winters brought penitence, and the short, white days were gasps of breath between the long nights.

The ground was hard in the chicken-run. The midden was crisp with frost. Maurice climbed on the roof of the dynamo, and parcels of snow fell down. The leaves that had clogged the sluice were gone, turned to pulp under the ice.

In the hen-house the hens nudged near to the old man to keep him warm. Maurice climbed the slats, and I followed him. Aunt Thelma had been down to the chicken-run on a tour of inspection, and had looked at the frozen burn, and stamped her feet by the forests of dead willow-herb, which were powerless now, like a child's rusting spears. She hadn't seen the old man when she looked in the hen-house. But a white hen had flown out at her, and she nearly slipped on the frozen chicken shit on the ground.

Maurice crawled out of the hen-house again. We went up the garden. Under a blackcurrant bush, which in the summer before Aunt Zita came had leaves that smelled strong and sweet, a snowdrop stood alone in the thorns. Maurice picked it and held it up to the light, its petals and its green scribble. We walked up to the house with it, but by the time we were at the house the petals had bruised and fallen. The hardest of the winter was all around us, and it was no herald of the spring.

PART TWO

South

WHEN the north still lay in darkness, and there were rumours of spring from England, my mother packed her suitcases and my father stood on the front door-step, his eyes staring in a southerly direction. The fields he could see at the end of the drive were the blank white of swallow shit. A lightness in the sky came from hidden snow, and not from the first spring days, which flitted over the country below us like fire burning paper. We were too high, in the black chimney of the north, to take that early glow. On the walls of the house, which had turned the colour of soot, snow and rain fell relentlessly.

My mother packed her clothes with little bags of dried lavender squeezed between them. Aunt Thelma had gone, and with her the Christian festivals which had never been welcomed in the north, and she had left behind her the hard truth of the unending winter: hills that hung over the valley like axe over block; mountains petrified in a mould that would last another iron age. The anvil of the year had turned. Aunt Thelma's lights, and the lacy jabot she wore at Christmas Eve, and the candles she put up around the manger in the hall, had melted and gone. The star which had guided the wise men shone coldly down on us, but no infant could have survived its rays.

My mother held the lavender bags up to her nose before she buried them in the case. Even in their dim colour the flowers bore witness to forgotten gaiety. The summer was prepared to give blues and reds and mauves and marigolds, and my mother was afraid that this might never happen again. For winter paid us hand over fist in the stark colours of economy. Once Aunt Thelma's garlands had been thrown out, and jaws of ice had bitten them, and the golden straw she had put around the manger had turned to a frozen nest on top of the midden, we saw in the landscape only the bare necessities of distinction. The white sky came down over the crests of the white hills. The white hills yielded to a stripe of brown before going into flat, white fields. And the trees, of the same grudging brown, stood without shadow on the white slopes of the hills.

This state of affairs went on for a long time before my father and mother decided to go south. They endured the death of the Christmas roses, and the growth of the Lenten roses, with their petals of sacrificial purple, in a land that detested icons. They watched every day the light grow heavier and more desperate, as if the new year were trying to drag the house and valley into the new season, and the burden was proving too much for it. They would turn to each other at the barely visible meals, and say: 'There isn't even anything in the greenhouse this year.' And my mother, after eating the winter food, would go to her room and open books of paintings of countries of the sun.

While my mother looked at orange hills painted by Cézanne, and the blue that fell across them in bolts from the sky, the hills outside folded to monochrome, and the mist in the valley became impenetrable. The house began to prepare itself for our going. Minnie went through the empty rooms on the top landing, shooing away the winter's crop of dead flies and the last, lingering presences of Aunt Zita. A taffeta skirt might stick out of a cupboard, and a pointed shoe. Minnie would hear wind in the chimneys when there was no wind to move the air over the house. And she would see, in the spotted mirrors it was never worth cleaning, the yellow turbans of Aunt Zita's grotesque night companions, and the cut diamonds Aunt Zita wore when she flew off to the ball. Even the corridors seemed determined to confuse rooms and conceal their destinations. Under skylights of rain they snaked and twisted, and Minnie would find herself slap up against a boxroom door or led treacherously down back stairs to an unimaginable scullery. When she found herself again, the passages were more narrow and secretive than before. They looped and double-turned, and produced cul-de-sacs of identical rooms where Minnie wrung her hands at the dust. Women with long necks and dressed as milkmaids stood in black and white prints on the walls. Their faces showed nothing, not even the ignominy of years spent in rooms that appeared only when the house was about to be abandoned. They held wooden pails, to conjure the illusion they were going to milk their porcelain cows, and the pictures hung askew, so that when Minnie, in her trembling rush at the top of the house, tried to set them straight, buckets rocked in elegant hands and blisters of milk showed up on the paper. In the yellow and green fields of their eternal summers, the first iron bridge of the Industrial Revolution hadn't yet cast its shadow. These women had no right to be in the house built by my father's grandfather: he must have brought them in to give himself a sense of ancestry: these haughty women, disguised as humble milkmaids, were the paradox of his own humble origins and princely disguise.

Uncle Ralph, disturbed in his winter cocoon by Minnie's attempt to get the house under control, to lock up the top floor so that none of its ghostly occupants could do damage while we were away, came out at the sound of her rattling keys and stood angry on the landing. My father wanted him to move downstairs in our absence, as if our trip to the south could somehow be echoed by Uncle Ralph's descent of the staircase to the lower floors. My father felt uneasy at leaving Uncle Ralph alone at the top of the house, that he would sway like an ungainly bird in the wind and fall from his winter perch at the coming of spring. Uncle Ralph always refused any blandishments. When my father built an electric train system in two adjoining rooms on the ground floor, knocking holes in the wall for a tunnel, Uncle Ralph went there only for an occasional visit. He played punctiliously with the trains as if to thank my father for the trouble he had taken, and we would hear the hoot of the miniature express and thunder of carriages over points followed by Uncle Ralph's deliberate march to the spiral stairs that carried him upwards. If greater efforts were made to dislodge him, he climbed away out of sight into a hidden boxroom. There, he would stumble over swarms of sleeping bees, and curl up in old saddles on the floor.

The house smelt of wax for days before we went to the south. Bees suddenly appeared under curtains and in corners. My mother brushed them away. Their drone in the hidden attic was as much of a threat to her as the roar of fire. For she feared that when she came back, after her longed-for journey, the bees would have built a great white labyrinth round the house, and Uncle Ralph would be hardly discernible, peering out at us from his window in the comb.

The south where Uncle Rainbow lived wasn't the orange south of my mother's picture books. It was the south of our own country, and trains took us through the night, against the magnet pull of the mountains, bursting out at last into the night glare of the Midlands, and running in the final drop into an intense green. My father and mother lay in their tiered bunks like stone crusaders. They showed no trace of anxiety at being drawn from the strength of the hills and made to float without defence in an unknown land. Fingers of cold came in on them in their swaying tomb, a quiver of ice arrows to bind them to the north, but they slept on, dreaming of spring. Before the howl of the furnaces, when the country was still hills, the flat white of the implacable winter outside came in through the window in a smell of unwashed basins. The absolute emptiness of the swelling and fading land must have made them think of the country they had left. Yet my mother and father failed to be drawn into the night, under the northern stars. For all the iron persuasion, and the severe necessity of the winter they had known, dreams of flowers and pale blue skies were stronger. Under my mother's lids lay a flickering tapestry, where the trees were just dancing into green.

Warnings of our imminent departure started to appear in the house in the north for some days before we left the valley and went to Uncle Rainbow's. Minnie, puzzled and defeated already by the clamming up of the top of the house, and by the forgotten kitchens slung across landings, where she would think she saw skeletal feasts, black bread held in beckoning fingers, found herself in the downstairs rooms caught up in clouds of butterflies. Straight from my mother's longing for the south, they flew out of cupboards and dropped limply to the floor before going into flight. They crept into the long room where Aunt Zita danced alone when she was courting the north wind, and spread out a million skirts of silk and polka dot. Minnie could see every dress my mother had worn, and some of the old ball-dresses Aunt Zita took from camphor wreaths at the top of the house. She waved her mop at them, but they only rose higher until they became sparks of iridescence in the lights. My father never referred to them. Even when a pair of blue wings hung over his place at the breakfast table, and he looked anxiously for a moment out of the window to see if an Asian landscape lay there instead of northern rain, he said nothing. Corners of his wife's long-discarded dresses animated the house. And as they came with such an intense longing for heat and colour, there was a softer feeling. But the accounts had to be got ready. Reports came in of sheep stranded in snow. The butterflies fell by the windows of the long room, where they had been trying to fly through glass to join the deadly whirl of the snow-flakes. Minnie picked up the shreds of material and put them on a table. They made a patchwork that has been ripped apart, and spelt the coming disintegration of the house.

My mother must have known her journey to the pleasures of the south would be dangerous. She knew the winter was like a wild beast by April, and that Aunt Zita, grown huge in its caress, roamed the house unrestrained by my mother's presence. When the trip to the south was over, the house was inspected for damage. Aunt Zita had left the stain of her black shadow on the walls of the upper rooms. Her teeth had crushed the chimney-stacks, and bitten away the slates on the roof. Where the north wind had come to collect her, it had chafed against the side of the house and broken windows in its terrible impatience. It had pawed the ground, and stampeded flowers and bushes. Yet even the knowledge of these disastrous couplings made little difference to my mother's determination to escape. She locked her room, but it was a pointless act. Minnie refused anyway to come into the house when it was in the grips of the last of the winter. Aunt Zita could go wherever she pleased, and left bat droppings and streaks of soot carried by her fingers to bedspread and chairs, ready for my mother's return.

When the mist in the valley was so intent on concealing any possible change in the year that it made new shapes from the larchwood, building cities and chimneys of mist, the collection of shells in my mother's bedroom began to glow with her unspoken longing for the south. The shells stood on a table in my mother's bedroom, under a window that looked out on the mysterious archaeology of the clouds. Their fleshy lips gaped at the grim scene. From roseate, polished depths the memories of hot seas rose to haunt my mother. It seemed literally incredible that such things could have been thrown carelessly by Nature on a beach. And there was also something scandalous about the colour: my mother's fingernails, which she painted to the same bright flush, fluttered in the room beside the shells and seemed to taunt the constricting skies outside. It was the colour of pure frivolity; of the flamingo cherubs which might be found, to the consternation of the north, if the heavy skirts of the mist were pulled back and back. My mother stood at the window in the greyness that would shade into night, and held the shells to her head. She heard the sound of the sea, and the rush of the train as it took us to the south. The cowries, pointed and dappled, she left untouched on their stand.

These shells, which took on all the vibrancy of space at the time of our leaving, flew ahead of us to the south and became embedded in the ceiling of Uncle Rainbow's dining-room. They were paler, and had been washed over in sickly colours, yet it surprised me always to find them there, when I had thought them alone in the empty house in the north. Their pink mouths were open to our gaze. The cowries, with their interior spirals as defeating as the geometry of the house we had left, were ranged on the ceiling like missiles. Uncle Rainbow would look up at the coral reef over his head as we ate. Some of the shells were tiny and green, emerald buttons. The coral lace, spread in fans, had turned yellow with nicotine. And Uncle Rainbow would say, turning to my mother at the table:

'Did I ever tell you about my last visit to Mauritius?'

In the south, passive listeners to our conversation, these shells from remote seas made no threat to the country outside. The country, deceptively and violently green, needed no provocation. But at first, when I sat in the dining-room in the air that was like breathing in a burrow of long grass, I thought it was as tame at Uncle Rainbow's as it was wild in the north. I knew nothing of the burst of spring. The faces of blossom I saw nodding at the window I thought only gentle and fragrant, in their reassurance of the mildness of the south.

Before we arrived in the room under the shells, when winter and the north crouched behind us and the grey land had gone into fields made green by spring, my mother pulled up the blind in the train and began to wash her face. Cows looked in on her, and new lambs. In the small towns we went through, people rising in the morning saw my mother go past, and raise her towel to her cheeks, and then she had fled from their room into the long, flashing windows of the street. A boy practising a trumpet in a window saw her, and caught her for a moment on the end of a brazen note. And housewives shaking rugs saw her. In the north, my mother had looked out on nothing. Here, everything looked in on her. Nature watched itself with extreme con-centration, and drew us into its self-conscious acts.

Uncle Rainbow was my father's cousin. His family had lived a long time in a house in a maze of tall hedges that let off puffs of yellow dust at the hand of the intruder. The hedges went up to within a few yards of the house, and in the spring the flagstones at the centre of the maze, which held and protected the house even further, sparkled with new rain. Bright blue flowers shot up out of the crevices. As my mother and father, disappearing from time to time in the lineaments of the maze, came up nearer to their goal, to the oak door which would finally take them in to Uncle

Rainbow, the window ledges on the upper floors let off a fusillade of white pigeons. The air was heavy with their wings. The windows, no longer watched and guarded, showed very dark over the bowed heads of my mother and father as they walked on the wet grass of the maze.

The searching eyes of the outside world had caused Uncle Rainbow's house to turn into a succession of boxes. In defence, each room and staircase fitted neatly into each other, with hinges and grooves that flew open when the house expanded and Uncle Rainbow, attended by Letty, made his occasional walks. This Chinese arrangement gave the house a closed-up look, and even on the more innocent days, when the boxes were sprawled like a child's building bricks over the lawns, or on moonless nights when they hummed with music, it was impossible to forget how forbidding and stacked-away it could appear. From the conjunction all round the house and gardens of the first ancient roads, and the henges of wood and stone which first gave shape to man's seeing mind, and the woods where the first human acts had been committed and recognised, the house was forced to protect itself. The hall had a filmy air, as if it might be obliged to disappear at any moment. Even Uncle Rainbow's extraordinary treasures, collected from a life of wandering the world, seemed to suffer under the attack of this vortex of the south. There was no question of animation here. The house boarded itself up against the power of spring. It could provide no memories, or returning spirits: only the eyes, fierce as bluebells against the window, transfixed it for ever in a passive and helpless state.

My mother, though she was used to the shrieking winds and violences of the north, fell easily into the muffled tones and silence that smelt of crystallised fruit which hung on the landings at Uncle Rainbow's. From the moment she said: 'Well Letty, here we are at last. How nice to see you', she visibly gave herself to the house. Her eye went in pleasure round the objects trapped all over the world and here displaying their inability to harm anyone. The more exotic, the more disappointing Uncle Rainbow's relics were: a shark's head, with pointed teeth more frail than the white petals of the flowers outside; a great straw suitcase from which flowed Eastern silks, and from which, because of the paralysis set up inside the house by the growth of the spring, the silks refused to flow with grace and excitement. My mother nodded to show her familiarity with all of Uncle Rainbow's odd collection. She stepped firmly into the house, and it fitted round her. In it, she sat and sewed with Letty, in the room the colour of an unripe apple behind the dining-room. She wore a calm, abstracted expression. For just as the cruel winds of the north had provoked her into anger and resentment, the dynamic workings of the southern spring seemed to bring her peace. She was both engaged in them and beyond them, observer and beneficiary. Letty would prick her finger as she sewed, and my mother would look from the droplet of blood to the white cherry blossom that stood outside the window in absolute stillness. Letty would smile slightly. But my mother, who had known Letty for years — Letty, who seemed never to grow any older, who had looked after Uncle Rainbow since he was a boy, noticed nothing. She trusted Letty completely, equating her with the bland cooking that appeared on the table three times a day, the sponges and junkets and white potatoes, and with the quiet, artificial rhythms of the house.

Uncle Rainbow's house was enfolded in the centre of the world. The old, magic roads that went off to Glastonbury in the west and to Stonehenge in the north, pinned the house in its maze by the long water-meadows. The beginning of time was still heavy in the air, which even in spring was thick and smelt of water. Over the downs, unmarked by the pictography of barley or wheat, there ran rough traces, worn by the dragging of stones. Men had dragged stones, to build their dial to the watching sky. But these ways, no more than a charcoal smudge from the windows of Uncle Rainbow's house, went as deep and narrow in the earth as the groove from the keel of a ship. When the world was water, and the downs were a green, running sea, ships glided over them and let down the stones on to the ocean bed. There they grew, into a city of grey walls and fish darting about amongst them, as bright as window-boxes.

Uncle Rainbow's ancestors had made bows for the battle of Crécy, from the giant yews on the hills. The house they had built was fortified, but it had long ago fallen and been built and rebuilt, an endlessly shuffling succession of boxes and cubes. In its chosen spot it invited, and was unable to avoid, the coming in and passing over of every message in the cosmos. From a satellite up by the moon, bands of pure colour would dance into Letty's sitting-room and become people and shapes of her own world. Sunk in the swamp from which life first emerged, the house held its latest occupant with the tenacity of a shell. Uncle Rainbow, knowing the dangers of his position, led so quiet a life that even when my father was there he seldom took him as far as the giant yews. The house might have been overcome by the time he got back. In the villages which lay in the flanks of the downs, the stone buildings were all pointed in the direction of Uncle Rainbow's family house. Pylons stood along the downs, ready for the stride which would knock both Uncle Rainbow and his house into the ground. And as Letty slept, in her bedroom under the eaves, swallows flew about the house in a circle, and perched on the telegraph wires to feel the stream of voices running under their feet.

My father always found the first days of his visit hard to

bear. He wandered about, trying to define both the house and himself, and Uncle Rainbow, in some sort of recognisable proportion. He went into Letty's sitting-room, where Letty and my mother were cutting out recipes, and pushing knitting into wicker baskets, and stood uncertainly by the fireplace. He saw on the mantelpiece a saucer of conkers, still polished brown, which Letty had collected in the autumn from the big tree outside her window. He looked out at the big tree and saw the buds bursting and swelling. And in that glance he showed all his astonishment at the spring. He opened the window sometimes, and leaned out to touch the buds, and drew his hand back in as if it had been bitten. The saliva stained his fingers. He had to endure Letty's laughing at his hand which he held like a paw as she scrubbed, and at her knowledge of the gallop of seasons that went by in his mind at the sight and touch of the leaf. He saw the first dazzling green, and then the white and red candles, and the heavy shade they gave when the leaves darkened and spread. In the turn of the year, with the fat brown nuts Letty liked to rub against her shirt, he saw the coming of death. But he said nothing, only went from the room to wander the house again, or out to the flagstones to look at the flowers that came up every year between them, in the cracks.

Uncle Rainbow lay most of the day in his room, on a bed covered with spotted scarves. There he talked in a desultory way to my father, but his eyes often fell shut, and my father, compelled to sit in silence on a gold chair near the bed, allowed the house to stretch, expand, reduce and add to itself in the absence of mind of its owner. Sometimes a gallery of rooms appeared, each room leading off the last, and my father strolled in them. He saw that one room contained only a harpsichord, which gave off a melancholy sound, and that outside were yew trees, reminding him of the north. In another room, panelled in oak and empty except for one leather chair, he sat and looked out at an unfamiliar garden. The rooms moved and subsided and in their shifting he thought he heard a scale of laughter. He never knew if Letty was laughing – at him, at his impotence in the face of the activities of the spring, and the eyes that stared in at the house, from trees and grass and lilac, from the raindrops that settled on the windows – or whether the sound came from the harpsichord, long after the rooms had gone away.

On the days when it had rained early in the morning, my father was particularly restless in this house where nothing spoke to him of his past. He went on to the wide landings, and looked out at the green wash over the downs. The smell from the poplars made him think of illness. The river had spilt on the grass again, and coots paddled in the grey water. Behind my father, arranged in an iconography of his life, stood Uncle Rainbow's most important possessions. The silks from the East gave off a sharp tang in the hours before anyone was about. Old photographs, crushed in frames of enamel water-lilies, had faded to the point of extinction, so that only an eyebrow of the sitter remained, or the sweep of a chin above a collar. Uncle Rainbow's letters and diaries, written in inks that became stronger in colour with each renewal of the spring, the sepia of the early entries turning as brown as earth, blues and greens intensifying and bursting from the page in a floral calligraphy, lay in leather trunks at my father's feet. The words confessed, boasted, and implored: my father stood motionless, in a dawn which had too little and acid a light for the space allotted it, and cursed the heavy weight of the south. In his mind, even the trees were buried in snow. Only the tops were visible, the straggling hairs of a brush dropped by the racing wind.

In that half-light, while my father still dreamed at the

window, he saw himself go out infinitesimally small into
the mists of the garden. Crocuses hung over him in imperial
canopies, the purple edges chewed by birds. In the cracks
between the flagstones were ruined temples and tombs. He
went under the yews, which held up the sky with their
enormous branches. The mists cleared, and the first sun
tipped the world upside down. Chandeliers stood in the
grass, and cloud gardens were blown across the sky. My
father walked into a city of crystalline water. The seven
colours of the spectrum made the shimmering walls. When
the sun came down it was as solid as gold, and the cities of
glass melted. The first shadows of the yews fell on the
brilliant green. Then my father went back to bed, triumphant at the sunrise and the contracting time to breakfast.
Still tiny, he climbed into the bed that smelled of sleep. And
he waited, while the sun's yolk poured in under the curtains,
so yellow that my mother's eyelids twitched and sparks of
gold flew in her sleeping pictures of the spring.

I knew my father took up his position on the landing in the
early morning in the hope that this would stop me from
going out to see what Letty and Uncle Rainbow did when
they left themselves behind in the house. He stood over the
entreaties of Uncle Rainbow's past, the violet dashes and
brown, faded exclamation marks that looked as if swords had
been thrown between the sentences. Some of the envelopes
on the floor had a scarab of sealing-wax on the stiff paper.
My father looked down in distaste at these emblems of the
split second of excitement, the moment when the heart
stops for news or words of love. He kicked them aside to
stand closer to the window. When I ran across the grass in
front of the house, I saw his round eyes at the pane, looking
mournfully out. He was a snail who has climbed by mistake
into a conch: the pink spiralling chambers that lay behind

him were Uncle Rainbow's, not his, and with his northern-ness removed from him he appeared baleful and ill at ease. His finger stubbed the glass, and he stumbled on the shifting piles of letters under his feet. Nuts of sealing-wax cracked, giving a scarlet dust.

Uncle Rainbow, although the recipient of those long-dead letters, had few marks of distinction. The house, and the deep gardens, and the woods where spring came every year, were indifferent to the nature of the incumbency. They had seen so many versions of him, in the long gener-ations since the first building and fortifying of the house, that when one puff of life went, and another came, it was no more than the shedding of a lizard's skin. That was why, at supper in the early spring days, when the lights were on in the dining-room, and reflecting in on us from the windows like the eyes of tigers in the garden, my mother would catch her breath at the sight of Uncle Rainbow. From the portraits above him and around him on the walls, he had taken an eye, a twitch under the cheekbone where the artist's hand had trembled with his brush, a left shoulder higher than the other and narrow and arched as a shoe-horn. The portraits, yielding their secret, genetic information, imparting their idiosyncracies to Uncle Rainbow, became bland, and also forbidding.

No one asked, when Uncle Rainbow's insignificant life had blown away, whether the house would have to go empty at last. For Uncle Rainbow's one mark of distinction from his forebears was precisely his refusal to continue them. The house and land demanded for their survival this continuation. In the spring they brought forth the origins of life to assail Uncle Rainbow. Tired and pale as he usually seemed in our visits, he was fighting them ceaselessly. My mother was probably unaware of this, and would have treated him with less glancing scorn if she had known the powers of resistance

Uncle Rainbow needed to stop himself from being repeated amoebically in every room in the house.

In the earlier part of our visit, when the chestnut buds were swelling and spring was still racing underground, my mother watched Letty closely and sat with her a long time at night. She was afraid that Letty might grow and fill the house. Then, thick, satiny limbs would entwine on the stairs and from Letty's vast body, pressed deep against landings and windows, a litter of living things would jump out. Letty's breasts swung, as she handed bread sauce with the chicken, and my mother looked on with a slight frown. On these evenings, we sat too long with the curtains open in the dining-room, and in our anticipation of spring became ourselves a lit shrine in darkness: the curious eyes outside which pressed in on us saw our odd assortment: the icon Uncle Rainbow's uncle had brought back from Constantinople, with its downcast eyes and inexplicable grief; the portraits of red-faced men in white wigs; and the living family group at a table under a constellation of shells. When Letty went to close the curtains, against the gaze of these nights of spring, her buttocks moved together amicably, and my father's eyes fell on the divide. He grew thoughtful, and turned to Uncle Rainbow with some sudden remark. But Uncle Rainbow was as studiously looking away from Letty as my father was unable to stop himself from staring. Uncle Rainbow chose always to examine the picture of hills and cattle that hung in the corner furthest from the door. Thus, he wouldn't even see Letty as she came and went, bringing with her smells of new carrots and the acid smell of spring as it crept along the corridors outside. He looked only at the watering-place where the cattle had gathered, and the thin stream that wound down from the brown hills.

For all the long sewing evenings my mother spent with Letty, and the vigilance of my father amongst the opened letters on the landing, Letty went from her room before the beginning of day, and I followed her. In that chaos of darkness, when the spiky flowers in the cracks in the flagstones nipped the toes like pincers, and the tops of great beeches floated slowly in convoy towards the downs, she walked with purpose, drawn to the source of water in the woodland like a thirsty dog. I soon learnt to go after her, by sliding down a slope of thatched roof under my window, and when I leapt the last feet on to the drenching grass I had only to cross one estuary to catch up with her before she went into the trees. It was surprising, even then, that my father didn't wake. Under his room, and directly in the path I had to take to be with Letty, stood the house on stilts where the white doves, going down lazily from the window sills at sunset, slept until first light. As I went barefoot under them, there were coughs, and the sail flap of wings. In the blackness, the invisible white bodies made a soft whirring. Then, as the birds crowded in again, the struts of the house groaned with the weight of the ringed and scrabbling feet.

In the wood, the river was buried. Its course could be seen by the trail of bright moss that hugged the hidden banks. In the clearings in the wood it came up in a green fizz. Letty went with it, feet magnetised by the pull of water under the earth.

Letty lay by the side of the pool. Above, the trees made an arch that was endlessly broken by wind. The moon, pale in the dawn sky, came down through whipping and coiling branches. Its face was shaken by the wind on the water, and went off in splinters into the mud. I stood by a tree, with my back against the trunk. Knobs on the bark, where limbs had fallen or been lopped, dug into my spine. I looked up at the sky, and I looked at Letty, as she lay still by the mouth of the cave. In the first days of spring, when Letty lay abject by the deep pool, legs straddling the buried river and head down in the mud, it seemed as if the cave might never grow by her side. Winter, which had laid down a carpet of yellow aconites and snowdrops in the dead leaves of the wood, had a stranglehold under the show of gaiety. With its iron flatness it held down the earth. The cave would never come up from the deep waters of the pool, and the spring would be throttled, buried alive under the old year's weight.

The winter trees had their own laws. The dancing flowers at their base were a short feast, enough to show that winter could dictate its pleasures. And they held their grim parody of life, too: in the branches, locked into shapes of faces and eyes, were the green men of the forest. Skeletal smiles were etched on a sky the colour of slate. Balls of twigs, thickly mashed, made heads no bigger than pygmies. Winter had its own citizens. Until the end it resisted the spring.

When winter finally succumbed, and leaves seized the flanks of the most impregnable trees, the grinning men left their branches and went to church on the downs. From columns in the transept, stained green as moss, the foliate faces looked down in laughter. Children, dragged to a service of Harvest thanksgiving, would look up at the pagan smiles set in stone. It was possible that one year, at the ending of the world, winter would conquer spring. Then the ancient faces would stare down for ever at the pool, and the cave always submerged, and Letty lying as a lifeless sacrifice, with a belly as flat as the iron armour of the year.

In those first mornings when I followed Letty to the pool, I understood why my mother tried to keep her from leaving the house, and why my father stood in the detritus of Uncle Rainbow's past, his only hope that he would catch us one day. I would grow and become as vast as Letty, and if he did capture us, we would only wilt in his hands. For what could he do with us? And I knew, despite my mother's longing for the spring and her coming south to meet it, that she too resented the lurch forward into time. There was a longing for standstill, for fear of the feel of the world turning under foot.

My father disliked the first signs of spring, the smell of swamp that Letty brought into the house after her morning excursions, the heave, away from law and order, from winter's graveyard tidiness. He stood on the landing in the half-light, listening to the faint drone of motorbikes on the downs. Local gangs, racing home after a night on the town, scorched the roads around the old Stones. He belonged in a half-lit world, where spring reduced him to creaks and aching of joints, and where the future, unconcerned with Earth's prospects for the new millennium, made composite men and sent them out to space.

In the house, Letty was firm and brown, with the tread of a hen. Soft bags of knitting fell from her lap when she rose, and pins slid from her hair, which was always brown. In the woods, I watched her as she went down in the slime by the side of the pool. It seemed that another woman grew beside her in the mud, and with enormous limbs overcame and subsumed Letty. The pool waited for the first splash, of the creature as it went to the depths. There, in a gloom thicker than the winter night, not even a leaf could stay, rotting. All went to mineral, to the beginning of a world without life. From those stones and boulders Letty had to rise, to drag herself to the mouth of the cave. As the ripples went out from her body, the light began to show through the trees, and the pool, like an eye hidden in the bushy woods, wept at the first rays of the sun.

In the later part of the morning, when my mother wanted to walk in the garden, I persuaded her to come into the woods, and through them to the first slope of downs under the pylons' legs. I wanted to see whether the cave, which formed in the shadows of night, was still there, or whether the sun, scouring the woods with a fiery besom, had chased it away from its dank spot by the side of the pool. My mother stood in the leaves under the trees while I crept round the small expanse of water. Where Letty had been, with her back as fat as a seal's in the pond, there were a few twigs floating. The cave was half gone, no more than a denseness of air between trees. I penetrated what had been its floor: a mulch of leaves, the colour of onion skins. And I walked along a runnel in the ground, where an ancient ship, on its way to the aquatic cities of stone, had gone into harbour. I wanted to see the furthest recess, where Letty crawled out of sight as the sun went higher, and where I had never dared to go.

'If this pond was a little bigger, it would have been nice to have a boathouse here,' my mother said.

Wind and sun together had taken away the mysteries of the cave. The sun had rushed in there, to whiten the walls and then dissolve them altogether, to paint Letty's diurnal face on her and send her back to house and duty. The wind had whipped up the leaves, hiding the last traces of Letty's altar. A thrush hopped in the sacred places. My mother grew impatient, pulling away from the pool towards the downs. The trees, which in their tattered winter coats of green moss failed to impress my mother, seemed thinner on the ground at that time of the day. We soon left them, and climbed to the crest of the downs. We stopped, looking down at the trees, and the garden sinking to the river beyond, and water meadows where cows stood without feet, marooned in the spring floods. My mother nodded, satisfied. 'It's a late spring,' she said. And then, remembering she had come south in the longing for spring, remembering the coral reefs and purple evenings that had haunted her in the north, she pointed at the trees below us. A fuzz of pale green hung round them. In their subjection to the coming summer they stood neatly below us, with the heads of obedient school-children tied in green ribbon.

When we arrived in the garden, my father came out to say it was time to eat. As we went past, I saw the buds were bigger on the chestnut tree outside Letty's window. Nearly free of their armadillo shell, it would take one more wriggle before they could explode into leaf. But the green men had gone from the branches at the defeat of winter. The trees sighed in the wind, bowed down already with deckings and loadings to come.

At the time most hated by my father, when spring hadn't yet got properly under way, and Letty seemed every day to grow bigger and vaguer, Uncle Rainbow stayed in his room; and when he did appear for meals he had a shrunk, wizened look, as if the last ounce of sap had been taken from his veins. I knew that Uncle Rainbow, or some semblance of Uncle Rainbow, went out at dawn, and prepared for the change in the year. It was impossible to know whether my mother and father knew this, and when my father sat at the table in the dining-room, staring out into the anxious gaze of the garden, there was a sense that everything was locked: that the trip to the south had been for nothing, that the host had no longer the strength to sit under the portraits of his forebears, and that the world, lacking a key to wind it up again, clung like a sticky burr to space. My father made a spiral from his apple peel and failed to meet my mother's eye. She talked of the primroses that were beginning to come up in the lanes, and he saw the lanes in a quadrille, dancing in flowered skirts at a court where the manners were foreign to him. Or he saw them as a maze, closing in on the yew hedges round the house, and he knew he would never escape. If the wind blew outside, he pinched the side of his nose and thought of the north. The north wind was racing now in the corridors at the top of his house, but what was blowing outside was south-westerly: it brought the fresh rinsed sky of the Azores and the flat fields of Southern Ireland, and my father yawned.

But the nights were drawing back, and Letty went earlier to the cave. As the green men settled in the churches, polyanthus shot up in village gardens and a bunting of yellow jasmine ran round the walls. Boys, hidden all winter in low rooms, came out with quiffs of hair malignantly shining. On bikes and scooters they dived in the shallow hills, and when they passed our gate they stopped sometimes, by the war memorial to Uncle Rainbow's brother, and stared in through the trees at us.

One of the boys, Victor, came through the maze of hedges and we played by the river in the garden, where it was too muddy for my mother to walk, or by the back door, out of sight of Letty in her window sewing. We listened by the pool in the woods for signs of the cave coming up again.

As well as the living, the dead stirred at the roots of spring. They jostled in the woods by the cave in the hope of re-generation. While Uncle Rainbow crouched in his room, or disappeared on journeys where it was not yet possible to find him, the portraits in the dining-room ingested his vital properties and went out wandering. They went in search of their own forgotten traces: of the one mark they had made for which they might be remembered; yet they were seldom successful, leaving only a garden and woodland more dis-ordered and trampled than before. Uncle Rainbow's brother, woken under the granite cross of the war memorial by the growl of Victor's engine, was particularly astonished – by the sameness of the place he had known half a century ago, and by the fact that the Great War had not allowed him to make any changes before he died. From a pencil sketch in the hall he looked bemusedly out, and when my mother, in her goings about the house, happened to pass him and catch his eye, she looked away in mild disapproval. The ridiculously short life span, the hopeful expression, gave her guilt in her own careful exultation at spring. On certain days, when the frame was empty and Uncle Rainbow's brother had gone to the woods, she pretended not to notice. But both she and Uncle Rainbow were relieved at the absence: the brother had been no more than a hiccup in the line, and he reminded Uncle Rainbow of the discrepancy in their earth and silken beds.

Some years, because my mother was afraid to arrive too soon and fret at the delay of spring, we came south as the folded leaves were prising open the buds. The dark, sour light round the house didn't deceive my mother then: she knew there was no sun to be seen, and the moon had gone too, and although she looked at Letty appraisingly, the fears of earlier days were gone. It was too late to stop the impending changes in the year. My mother unpacked sunglasses. My father, delighted at doing without the revulsion of watching winter's burial, and the bloody shoots it sent up into the apple trees, hummed in the house and read through piles of Uncle Rainbow's old newspapers. These announced forgotten wars and treaties: my father, looking out from time to time at the landscape stained red by spring, sighed at treachery. On the wide landing, or in one of the little-used rooms downstairs where Uncle Rainbow had hung his shells in baskets and nets, he could be found sitting in a Panama hat and holding an ancient newspaper. The house had become a beach, and these objects were his *trouvailles*. He was a northerner in the tropics. The knowledge of the imminent birth of the sun gave him more pleasure than the thing itself.

In the days when we had arrived late from the north, my mother took care to hide her disappointment at the lack of southern stars, the absence of tropical flowers, the meadows logged with water still silver in frost. She walked the house in her sunglasses, and picked her way among Uncle Rainbow's collections. The moon had gone from the sky, and the sun chased after it. Day and night were obscure and undivided. Only Letty's meals announced the time. There was talk of neighbours: they called at this blank stage of the year, as if they knew they didn't fit by rights into any real season: Uncle Rainbow muttered of getting a girl in to help. While my mother and Uncle Rainbow spoke the names of houses and their occupants, I thought of Victor. As there was no longer any way of knowing the time, I couldn't wait to see him. The village that looked as if it had been beaten by a broom into a corner of the downs held him close then. Neither winter nor spring. Victor stood pale by the door of his mother's cottage. It was impossible to tell whether he was going in or out; but his neck, rising from a bright white shirt, arched to the colourless sky.

My mother said she had heard from Letty that Victor had a sister who might help in the house. And she smiled at Letty as she said this. Letty looked back at her unsmilingly. A good dinner service would have to be brought from the cellar. From dusty plates entwined initials would appear. Glasses would have to sparkle, at just the time when there was no moon to come in and set them shimmering. They would stand, crystallised tulips of water, on a table as black and smooth as winter earth. I saw Letty sigh and throw glances at Uncle Rainbow. But he nodded at my mother and said:

'Why not ask the girl to come down for a week or two?'

The neighbours came, and sat under Uncle Rainbow's ancestors. They laughed very little, speaking mainly of threatened estates. Their coats were stiff, and when they hung in the hall they made a curtain that cut off the life of the fields and woods outside. Even the feel of the house was muffled. Imprints of complacent faces hung in the air after them, until Letty opened the windows and went from room to room brushing them away.

In the absence of sun and moon, the house took on the appearance of a luxury cruiser. A tinny piano could be heard every time Letty opened the dining-room door to go out with the plates. A Charleston record came intermittently, as if blown by a sea wind. Without real light from outside, the house manufactured its own: the guests had green faces, and the food looked dead and tasteless. Yet even in its new guise, things didn't go as they should. The music sounded as if the needle were going the wrong way on the track.

As the control just held, the neighbours ate off gold-rimmed plates and Letty poured wine from thin bottles. My mother and Uncle Rainbow looked anxiously about them, to see if any further transformations were taking place. The leaf and root features of Uncle Rainbow's ancestors were autumnal. They were in suspense for the changes to come.

My father, when persuaded to join the company, dressed in a dark suit and spoke in a solemn voice as if explaining bad news. While the guests complained of the weather and the dark, he saw the vanished planets in Letty's moving arse. A crescent moon was there, running slap up the middle of an orbiting sun. My mother rang the handbell incessantly, like a votary demanding the resumption of an interrupted mass.

Annie, Victor's sister, waited by the war memorial after

she had finished washing up the plates. She waited for Victor to come and get her, and in the evenings that were already longer he came from the village on his bike. His black, greased head was a blur above the white lamp. She climbed up behind him, and they went on the twisting roads over the downs.

Everybody and everything waited for the turn of the wheel. Then, spring would come. The house waited. On Doric columns in the hall, the frieze of serpents stopped their chase and waited to reverse direction. Uncle Rainbow and my mother waited. Under the shells in the dining-room they felt the gyre falter and stop. Letty waited. She laughed at my father's mournful stare, and at the eyes of guests averted from her muddy hands.

Uncle Rainbow disappeared often in these days of suspense. He left meals early, and stripped off the last vestiges of identity, and went out through a side door to the garden. I followed him to the river. Uncle Rainbow crossed a bridge over swamp, and the tributaries that lay hidden in the grass. He came to the river. The remains of a boathouse, built as an Oriental pagoda, stood behind him, and water filled it. On this floor of onyx a boat sighed, to the ripples of wind on water that came in like fans. Uncle Rainbow knelt on the bank. He stared intently at the mud, and the little round holes like buttonholes made by the worms as they went in and out. On the important tide a swan passed. I had seen the tall nest of twigs, further upriver, where the eggs, packed close together as bombs, lay waiting for the sun.

The first signs that water would burst everywhere within the next twenty-four hours came from Letty and my mother. The sound of the weir, usually no more than a faint rustle, seemed to emanate from Letty. My mother rising from her bath found herself covered in pearls of water, which clung stubbornly to her skin. The plates and cups my mother and Letty washed took on an indelible water mark. A salty smell invaded the house, and the pictures in the frames warped as sea air attacked the gilt.

Uncle Rainbow's river bank grew to a wide beach of pebbles. He crouched still, under a sky torn by wind. The blue air and racing clouds swallowed him, and sea birds danced wildly over his head. He looked up sometimes and stared out at the ocean. He scanned the waves, as if a message could be deciphered in the foam.

My mother and Letty paid no attention to the drama Uncle Rainbow was about to produce. They fussed round my father instead. My father had set up a deckchair, found in one of the collections and rotting in its fabric, on the landing where in earlier days he had stood at dawn and looked out. The window was open as far as it would go: my father, lolling like a passenger in his new enjoyment of the house, inspected the world through binoculars. They made port-holes of his familiar window, but he never said if he saw the sea. Letty and my mother never asked him. They brought up soup, and club sandwiches my mother was fond of making, and if they glanced at the window they nodded non-committally at the grey mist that could have been sea or land, the yellow gravel path just visible below.

Uncle Rainbow walked along the beach until he was dovetailed by mist. He went in sharp stones up to his ankles. Sometimes he picked up a smooth white stone and hatched it in his hand before letting it fly to the sea. I followed at a distance, and when he heard my feet on the pebbles he turned and looked uncertain. He might have been hearing his own echo. He searched below the high tide mark, on stones that looked as if they had been scalded by tea. Rags and rubbish clung to the broken concrete posts of the breakwater, and he poked amongst them with a stick. These posts had been put up to repel the enemy. Now a solitary wire straggled from the top of each but they still stood to attention, clutched by detritus. Rag skirts swelled round them in the tide and weed made slimy ribbons. To the thump of the waves the stone defenders danced with the rags which had been swept in on them.

Uncle Rainbow went down to where the sea was coming in, and the sea circled his shoes and soaked them without his knowing. In his wet shoes he tramped the city of the edge of the sea. The sea came in in arcades, and in single columns that shot up the beach and then toppled. In these shallow edifices, where tiny fish swam and black poppers of weed were embedded in the stones, Uncle Rainbow explored with caution. The water was treacherous, and dappled like the belly of a great, flat fish. It might rise up at the prod of his stick and bring the ocean down on our heads.

The sea hissed at Uncle Rainbow. He stood on the beach, thwarted. The stone heads of the sea tossed, and pounded down at his feet, and pulled back again, gasping, through combs of black weed. The mouths of the sea refused to answer him. From the stone mouths of the sea came riddles, impossible to understand, and spewings of foam.

My mother went up on the downs and along the road to the village and back again to the house, and she did this every day as if the constant circulation would exert the spring. I went with her, wishing I could play with Victor. But his motorbike, in the shed to the side of the garden, was dangerous and forbidden. My mother was afraid he would take me with him on a ride. As we passed the garden, and the house where Victor and Annie lived with their mother, she stared at the bike as if it had no right there. The neat beds that waited for wallflowers, and the raked path Annie walked obediently every day, were threatened by the black bike. It stayed in the shed like a crouching man, shoulders colossally padded and a narrow waist.

After the spring had come, no one remembered the last blank, unmarked day, when Uncle Rainbow brought the sea finally into the house, and the tide in Letty's pool rose, and the water covered us completely. In the bright rays of the sun, when the shadows from the hedges in the maze were black on the path, and the last drops of water blazed in the trees, we thought only of light, and of the summer that was opening out in front of us. In the last, dark day, we had looked up at the sky made of water. We never imagined we could be free of it.

The sea emptied into the sky when the earth tilted at the turn of spring. We lived under trees of dripping weed, and high in the sky, like a trail of stars, the keel of a ship would leave a wake of phosphorescence. Letty, deeply immersed in her pool, saw us only as reflections in the still water: a group of people distorted by the jolt of the season, under shells that grew over our heads.

In the cave, Letty lay and waited for the hour of birth. After it had come, and the day fell into marked divisions, we had as little memory of the past as of an eventless dream of water. My mother put on a bright lipstick and combed her hair. Letty had brought the sun, and a thin new moon which never left its place beside it.

When spring came, my father and Uncle Rainbow walked on the downs that had risen from the sea in the shape of lobsters. They congratulated each other on the coming of spring. Over them, in the pale haze from the sun, swallows flew to their nests. On the roads, smooth and black as the birds, Victor and his friends circled and dived.

My mother put on her sunglasses and stared straight up at the sun. She saw it coming out of the cave, bursting from Letty. In the garden she pulled in wonder at the chestnut leaves, which had flapped out limp from the chrysalis. The grass stained her shoes, and she came back into the house with green feet, as if she had been walking on a wet canvas. The white and red blossom began to affect my father. He sneezed, and tears ran out of his eyes. In the new brightness, the flowers and trees contained some intolerable knowledge, and my father pined for the north. The harmony of the south disturbed him. Flags of all colours waved together, and my father wanted the intransigence of the north, the one, stubborn view.

Uncle Rainbow and Letty ate green vegetables that came up in the garden. They were happy, in the bright sun they had made. Letty rose early, and my mother found her at the back door, pulling at the dandelions and coltsfoot that had come down in a shower from the sun. Letty always turned to my mother and said:

'Why not stay all summer this time? Don't go back so soon!'

Hot and yellow, the sun lay all day in Letty's arms. The brightness of the light crept into my father's mind and made him think of the future of the world. But he chose the dark. We drove to the station, and waited for the train that would take us to the dark again.

In the north, spring had hardly touched the trees and hills. It had come in pale, uneven waves, and then receded, leaving a faint wash over larch and elder. The dark came down in the evenings as if it never would give way to spring.